# A FEAST OF PUTRID DELIGHTS

## VALENTINA ROJAS

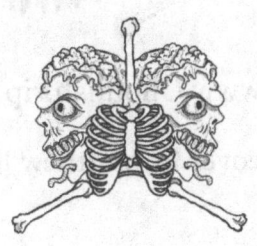

**Ghoulish Books**
San Antonio, Texas

**A Feast of Putrid Delights**
Copyright © 2025 Valentina Rojas

First Edition

All Rights Reserved

ISBN: 978-1-963801-09-5

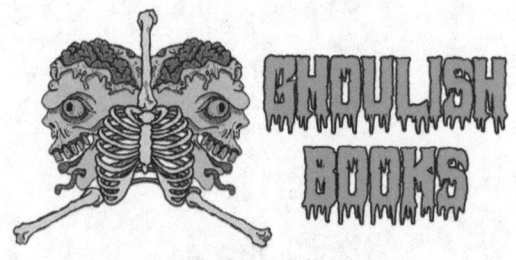

www.Ghoulish.rip

Front cover by Matthew Revert

# ADVANCE PRAISE FOR A FEAST OF PUTRID DELIGHTS

"When the price of peaceful sleep is a waking nightmare. Valentina Rojas' *A Feast of Putrid Delights* is a delightfully disorienting and grotesque descent into monstrosity."

—Cynthia Pelayo
Bram Stoker Award-winning author of
*Vanishing Daughters*

"In her debut novella, Valentina Rojas doesn't so much seat you at an ornate table and pamper you with a sumptuous course of delicacies. Instead she straps you to a chair, shoves a funnel in your mouth, and stuffs you."

—Michael Tichy
Author of *Behind Every Tree Beneath Every Rock*

"Reading *A Feast of Putrid Delights* is like being caught in an awful, restless dream. [...] A beautifully-realised nightmare, this is a confident debut novella with an ending that will haunt me for some time."

—Saoirse Ní Chiaragáin
Author of *Wax & Wane*

"*A Feast of Putrid Delights* is *The Vegetarian* without pulling punches. [...] Beautiful prose that lights up during scenes of violence that kicks off into one final scene of horror."

—O.F. Cieri
Author of *Backmask*

*To Eldar, who always believed.*

"*Now* a warning?"
—Helen Sharp, *Death Becomes Her*

I've been over and over it and the truth is, I don't think I will tell you exactly what happened, at least not now.

Part of my reasoning is selfish: once you tell people the big tragedy in your life, that's all they think of you. We can't help it. The event becomes your core, as if that one thing explains everything about you—a neat and tidy and digestible conclusion to your entire person. Sometimes that can be a relief, but more often than not, it's a curse.

All you have to know is there was a thing that happened.

And that I haven't slept since.

# PIXEL CLUB BOMBED: 5 KILLED, BOMBER PLEDGED TO "EXPEL DEMONS"

███ ██ CNR—

An American college student who'd pledged allegiance to a local anti-LGBTQ group set off a bomb which killed 5 people early Saturday at PIXEL, a gay nightclub in ████.

The bomber, Ethan "Teddy" Brockshield, 22, of ████ was interviewed by college psychiatrists in 2018 but was not found to be a threat, the FBI said.

After a standoff lasting three hours, while people trapped inside the club desperately called and messaged friends and relatives, police entered the building with an armored vehicle and stun grenades and killed Brockshield.

Parents of Brockshield say Brockshield was a "good kid" who stayed out of trouble and had "several gay friends." The investigation has uncovered journals where Brockshield wrote diary entries of his "struggles" with his own homosexuality.

Authorities say—

# PIXEL CLUB BOMBED: 6 KILLED, BOMBER PLEDGED TO "EXPEL DEMONS"

# ACT I

**WHEN YOU THINK** about it, delusion is the first thing diagnosed at the doctor's office.

*Everything's fine! There's nothing to worry about. Everyone experiences sleepless years like this.*

It's no use.

I've rehearsed my own story—the story that everything is alright—and am trying to explain this to the doctor when he stops me mid-sentence.

"How long have you gone without sleeping?"

"Let's see. Last full night of sleep was two days ago. But it isn't—"

He cuts me off again.

"When did this start?"

I blink.

Blue and red lights. A ringing in my ears. Bodies shuddering to the ground.

"Six years ago, I think."

"Right."

"On and off," I add, to lessen the severity.

"Hmm, I see. Well, I'm going to prescribe you some Ambien. Take one tonight and catch up on sleep. I'll recommend you to a sleep physician if it doesn't help, but let's give the old college try first. Okay?"

His question doesn't warrant an answer.

Before I know it, I'm scooted out of the room by the doctor's invisible hands to the receptionist's corner, to wait and pay the copay fee, then back into my hot-junk of a car.

No time to admit to the good doctor that this sleeplessness has been going on for years and that sometimes weeks go by without a wink of sleep. No time to tell him I'm *unnaturally* unwell. And, no time to protect myself against the consequences if he *does* end up believing me.

I crinkle the prescription into the glove compartment,

where it joins a lifetime of wadded-up, unused scripts. Could make a good side buck selling these. I look in the rearview mirror and shake my head. I promised not to do that anymore.

Another dead end.

I jam the key into the ignition and tear off into the serpentine highway.

The last good sleep I had was almost the death of me.

I was working at a little joint called Comma. Your typical, new-age chef nightmare. A historic creaky house-turned brunch spot, at the corner of Ellum and some new block of gentrified apartments overlooking a dirty dog park.

I'd start weekend mornings at 4 am, prepping containers of cyst-colored hollandaise sauce until I could smell it sweating out of my pores, and chopping fine potatoes (they had to be "fine" to validate the elevated dining prices) until Binder, a gruff New Jersey implant, appeared, breathing the odd critique down my neck.

Yuppies and college kids gathered at the door in large, fleshy bulges, waiting for a seat on our cramped patio. Plate after plate of glacial eggs, sausage links, and that damn hollandaise sauce zooming by us. We all turned a sick shade of puce by noon.

When our shifts ended, whoever wasn't on clean-up duty went looking for distractions for whoever wanted to pass the evening away. And naturally, I'd tag along—bored, expendable, the restless venom of youth pumping through my veins.

This evening in particular, I had no other place to go. Mika and I weren't speaking at the time. My aunt Jo was in Florida getting some experimental cancer treatment. So when Rody and Binder asked me to join them at their loft, I was game.

Binder's loft was a bright-white room on the second floor of a hipster development, sandwiched between a tattoo parlor and a noisy bar. Pretty generic all in all. Inside the elevator, a fresh paint smell lingered and I felt us all sharing a pre-high on our way up.

The narrow hallway of Binder's loft gave way to a messy bachelor pad. Mismatched IKEA furniture, a bulky record player, a collection of vintage framed t-shirts framed the unmounted television. The glass coffee table, with its marbled green base and spotless surface, was anachronistic, which spoke to an intentionality not apparent elsewhere in the room.

Rody swept his dark hair into a ponytail and knelt onto the faded rug. While we settled in, Binder went off and I heard the static hum of a television somewhere in the kitchen. Binder's hacks echoed against the industrial walls until he reappeared, his lumpy figure wobbling over to us with a plastic baggie tucked between two sausage fingers.

"Ladies first."

I didn't want to be a coward, so I pushed the apprehension out of my mind and snatched the baggie. There was a performative aspect to this ritual I enjoyed more than the drug itself. The placing, the camaraderie, and the instant moans of otherworldly escape shared among the participants. That and boredom, like I said– craving something to make the hours go by quickly.

I shook out two lines for each of us, which elicited a nod of approval from Rody, and a clap from Binder, who kept insisting this was proof he wasn't a "cheapo". Perched over the heavy glass, I snorted, instantly erasing the world around me. The capillaries on my cheeks felt flushed with new blood. Binder's laugh echoed around us. They both hit the lines in unison, letting out a gasp I knew only a few had heard before. Then my nose tickled something awful. Like an allergy attack gone mad.

The last thing I heard before blacking out was Binder whispering, *"fuck,"* as his large torso thudded to the ground.

I woke up days later to the sound of Mika's voice on the tail end of a phone call.

"Binder's fine. He's getting his stomach pumped but he'll live. Rodrigo too. The idiots."

"Good," I whispered hoarsely.

He turned to me, mouth gaped open like a fish.

"I got to go, honey."

In spite of my grin, everything hurt.

I could feel his lips on the hummingbird flutter of my eyelids as he leaned in. A kiss on each eye. My body went rigid.

He told me the gist of it while we adjusted my bed: the cocaine was laced with a new street drug. Something the kids called *Cloud*—a sedative some yuppie drop-outs had unleashed onto the market. On its own, it wasn't deadly, but in combination, weird shit happened.

A nurse swung by with a plate of goopy-looking food, admonishing me in an old southern tone about how I was lucky to be alive. I didn't want a lecture, so I just nodded along.

At the sight of the food, my stomach growled. I unsheathed a plastic spoon while Mika went on.

The drug part didn't interest me back then. At least, not in the way he assumed.

"Wait—you're saying I *slept*?"

"Yes, for two days."

I dove into the pudding cup.

"Mika! This is . . . "

My eyes burned from crying.

"I thought that whole thing was under control."

"If you think sleeping a full night every few weeks is under control, then sure."

"And the doctors? I mean, have you ever been to a specialist?"

"This is why I didn't tell you. Doctors aren't wizards, you know. Plus, they'll just think I'm a freak. Get all lab rat on me."

"So you have been . . . ?"

I rolled my eyes at him and scooped another mouthful of pudding into my mouth. The light cocoa flavor was replaced with a thick, congealed sludge. A combination of lard and that pink paste you get at the dentist's office. I couldn't swallow it, not after that smell; sewage cake and old menstrual blood. I spit it out on the plate and pushed the tray away.

"This shit is *rotten*."

Mika smirked.

"What did you expect? It's hospital food, *Chef*."

Except I wasn't *Chef* back then, and Mika liked to tease. It was something we daydreamed about. Well, Mika did, anyway. I hitched my dream alongside his, because it made sense. Because I was desperately trying to find an obsession we could share.

He handed me the juice box, which didn't quite taste like apple, and did little to rid my tongue of the unpleasant residue.

For a moment, expired food aside, it felt like the old days. The days before culinary school and the adventures of Mika and his shiny new fiancé. A little too much like the old days. I watched Mika's gentleness grow smaller in his eyes when his phone pinged, a message from his fiancé surely. Might as well change the subject.

"Do you know where I could get some of that Cloud stuff?"

"You gotta be fucking kidding me."

"To sleep! Sleep!"

Mika went on a tirade about having had to convince the nurses I was clean as a baby and would never have done that unless I was influenced, which I was prone to, and that rehab was not necessary. They couldn't force me, anyway, so they laid off after his explanation of my weak and gullible character.

"Don't do this to me again."

"No promises. The food here is pretty great."

That was a couple of months before Aunt Jo would pass, before I would quit Comma and leave bad habits behind, before Mika and I would open Iris together, and three years to the day after Pixel happened.

I thought about Cloud for a bit, I'll admit. But whatever had started in California died there, and after a series of crackdowns, Cloud was another fantastical magic dream needing to remain in the past.

Plus, I swore to myself I'd ditch the substances on my nighttime escapades, not on account of any moral reasoning, really. The thing about them was they made the lies hard to control, harder to recall, and I couldn't risk that. I was lucky enough that my first hospitalization happened with Binder and Rody, who had as much to lose as I did. So *Comma* became the end to a chapter, a scapegoat for a problem no one knew of. No harm, no foul. The same couldn't be said of Mika, being my closest friend, but at least I could keep a lid on how bad it really was.

Blink and you miss it.

A shudder of noises propels me back to reality. The radio, a blocky old thing, sits on the upper left shelf of my kitchen, blaring something about a new club downtown called—a pan clatters in the background and I miss the last part.

That's the thing about the sleeplessness. You miss things, lose things. Whole chunks. If a doctor had taken a CT scan that morning, they would have found Swiss cheese.

***Exhibit A:*** I spent a whole summer listening to music the last year of culinary school. Real sad stuff, complete with whiny male vocals. What can I say? It helped my dicing skills.

Looking back now, I can only remember the whole year in flashes: searing burns on my arm, how to poach an egg correctly, the right way to break down mushrooms (using the blade of a knife), lectures from instructors on culinary history, maddening creations eaten at midnight, but all of that takes second place to a dour medley of depressing acoustics. It's a blur. I should have listened to my first-year instructor who told us to cook in silence: *food has a sound and it is speaking to you.* Guess I am a slow learner. After that, I made a point never to listen to music again, especially while cooking.

There are a few other rules for sleeplessness: take copious notes, write a script for how the day has gone while waiting for the subway, layers are important, and always keep a pair of shoes at the door (protecting the feet while sleepwalking is important). Following that routine, I replay the morning events as I walk to the station making sure I don't forget them.

I park my car in a garage and board the subway at a quarter to eight, still flicking the crust out of my eyes. Crowds are bigger than usual, but it's nine in the morning–the second rush hour. The sleepless part of me watches as a woman with two small kids and a warm smile props open the door for me with her welly-booted foot. She gives me a nod while one of her kids glares. He's wearing a shirt with a mischievous looking lemur and blue sneakers.

When the subway train finally comes to a halt, a leak of acid from my tomato toast hits the back of my throat. The bodies empty out of the carriage, taking their heat with them. Random waves of piss hit my nostrils as we turn the corner—one lethargic, giant mass of flesh. I glance up at the towering buildings and imagine my small little body dancing beside them: a red-headed Godzilla.

The crowd disperses, no longer masquerading as some great ugly leviathan. I'm sick with nausea, which is not surprising. This is, after all, day five of no sleep.

Then my cell rings.

"Yeah?" I swallow hard, the acidity bouncing off my teeth.

"You sound terrible."

"I was at the doctor's office. Got one of those 24-hour bugs."

"Shit. Think you'll be good by tomorrow? I won't be able to open."

"Why not?"

"You're gonna laugh."

The pit in my stomach says otherwise but I respond with a flirtatious—

"Tell me."

"Uh, Hannah and I are going to a checkup. We get to see the baby today. Or you know, its underwater, alien-looking pictures."

"Oh!"

*"We"* means Hannah, "the fiancé", and Mika are more real than they were to me four years ago, when they first moved in together. She and the baby would come first. A distraction on the most important night of our careers.

"I know the timing is rough but it won't take too long. I've already talked to Raula about taking care of my stocks."

I reply with a mixture of *"That's so great"* and *"Don't worry about it."* Neither of which come out the right way. Our restaurant feels miles away, and all I can think of is how Mika has transformed—no, mutated—into one of those people who says "we" when talking about two distinct human beings. Cool, chic Hannah. Getting pregnant before the courthouse wedding. How alternative of her.

"You there?"

"Don't worry about it," I repeat again.

"It's still our night. This is important to me."

"Uh-huh."

*Click.*

The conversation haunts me the whole way to the restaurant district. I swear I see sonograms mirrored in the cloud reflections against the steel fish house—Mika's future baby, creaking in the sun. As tall men unlatch the metal gates facing the marina, I grow angrier and angrier. No matter how much I try, that silly girl from four years ago keeps rearing her big, ugly head. There are repulsive thoughts in my head I am trying to forget, but then again, that's also the sleeplessness. It makes me obsessive.

I hadn't planned on this emotional bulwark the day of the critic's visit. The insomnia churns the acid in my stomach like I'm about to puke. I take the tarps off the patio before I go inside. Above the evergreen tent, tiny Nunito font words glimmer in the light—Iris: fine American eatery.

I'm the first to arrive this morning, as usual. Mika, Lionel, Raula, and some of the crew usually straggle in around nine-thirty. The espresso machine, a cherry red Lavazza, wheezes into a small glass. I cannonball a double-shot into my already-acidified stomach.

I'm hunched over a clean counter, writing down the end-of-day reports I should have done last night with a bold, black Sharpie, when the door swings open.

"Boss, do ya ever go home?"

Lionel's soft, slurpy voice comes up behind me.

"Hey, Lionel. Food is on the counter."

Lionel slings his jacket over the table, smelling the yeast-infused air with a yearning "*hmmm.*"

"You *do* like your butter, Chef."

"You don't have to eat it."

"How can I resist?" he exclaims, plating himself a slippery yellow cod with kale and cannellini beans.

Raula and Gerri show up a couple of minutes later and we all break bread together. No one mentions Mika's absence. Still, Raula directs long glances towards me for the rest of the evening, a perpetual expression of pity. *Poor Antonia—has to watch her unrequited love pick someone else over her and then stand by and watch while they play happy family.*

I must be playing it extra cool because, at one point,

she comes by and offers up a sardonic commentary on the latest guests.

"See those kids out there? Spawn of Satan. The parents don't need a Bavarian truffle, no offense intended, Gerri— they need to *fuck*."

Gerri snorts and goes back to his truffle batter. I shoot her a meek smile, hoping Mika is too busy handling the steaks to overhear.

"Count your blessings, Chef. Mika's got a big head."

At the end of the day, I'm giving the crew my prepared speech about tomorrow being just "like any other night" when Gerri chimes in for Mika to tell us the 'big news.'

The whole crew is up in arms, banging pots and cheering until Mika acquiesces.

"Hannah and I are pregnant."

More cheers.

There's no place left to quell our excitement but The Blind Tiger—a mildly seedy, after-hours bar where food pirates destroy our livers with beer and unnameable plastic baskets of grease. The crew follows Mika out, and I'm left closing up shop.

So much for nothing changing.

Blind Tiger is a narrow building tucked between a laundromat and a Cash-Now store on the corner of the last ungentrified block near downtown. A proper hole in the wall, complete with *tchotchkes* from an assortment of Eastern European countries lining the shelves and all the weird junk you'd find in your grandmother's basement.

They have all the stuff cranky food service folks are hungry for at the end of the day: fried pickles, giant pitchers of beer, the classic American Peanut grab-bowl, and oddly enough—expensive bottles of Spanish wine. David Bowie and Elton John croon you into a stupor until you're so damn drunk you start believing you're Rocketman.

Jaime, the newest to our squad, orders us a double

pitcher at the bar, giving Lionel and Raula time to fully check him out. Creeps. The rest of us hunker down around a few tables as Mika plops in-between me and Lionel.

"Hey, Hannah had a rough day so I told her to meet us here. That okay?"

"Sure, Sure."

Lionel and Raula throw me a look. I wish I had laser eyes.

Hannah strolls through the door in her usual too-expensive-for-you artist garb, and greets me demurely. Another look from Lionel and I'm about ready to send him flying. *Control, control.* I order the crew a round and count the minutes until it's socially acceptable to leave.

"You're too pretty to go home, boss!" Jamie winks. I push a flight of whiskey shots his way, manipulating an excuse out of goodwill.

"This isn't carte blanche to come in tomorrow all fucked up."

The lot of them grin at me with the full glow of inebriation. Raula, Jaime, Gerri, the hostesses, Nadia and Marissa, Mika, and even Hannah.

"Yes, Chef!"

The last daub of twilight floats over the gas station when I pull in. I can see my breath in front of me as petrol shudders into the car. Behind the sign, the indigo sky gulps up the road. My head buzzes with the feeling of sleep—a ghost feeling, like an amputated limb.

Back at my apartment, I try desperately to sleep. Eyes shut in some kind of prayer for an hour, two hours, four. I try to build enough spit in my mouth to swallow the feeling of cottonmouth away, too tired to get up and go to the kitchen. The veins on my head throb, an invisible headache eating away at my thoughts, which are already fuzzy from the lack of sleep. I lean over and strands of hair get pulled into the curve of my neck. In a few years, the insomnia outfit of the day will be baldness. I try to cry but nothing happens. When I finally check my phone, it's 5 am.

I have no energy to go sit at a club or dingy bar, where I'll keep watching the door, haunted by the expectation that I'll eventually recognize one of the faces from Pixel. Except I don't remember their faces, not quite. Memory is like a dream now, a compilation of features where only the feeling of them makes sense.

And lying around won't do anything to help the insomnia.

On the bright side, early mornings in the kitchen are the closest I can get to bliss. When I arrive at Iris, it feels like I've never left. Clean counters, bright lights, polished cutlery, and pots gleam from every station. There are no strange odors in the air from marinating seafood in our fridge, or aged beef, no whiffs coming off the outdoor compost. Memory does not exist, and the future is a plate away.

I change into my chef apron to give the night its first ritual. An offering to the memory gods. Next, I polish up the dining area, in case the cleaning team missed anything. I notice there's still dust caught in corners of the carpet and spend the next half-hour on my knees with a couple of wet wipes and a handheld vacuum. I get hungry and raid the mini-fridge in my office. The fridge is tucked under a narrow corner, warm with the heat from my old Dell computer. Inside, the jars and containers are just the way I like them: description, prep date, three zig-zagged underlines. Next to the budgeting binders are Mika's journals. Curiously out of order. I pull one down and am suddenly filled with dread. A quick look over the menu for tonight sends me deep-spiraling. It's too basic, too overdone. I skim through the latest pages of Mika's journals. He's been obsessing over souffles lately. *Their upcoming pre-baby trip to France.* The journals are beautiful, works of arts in themselves. Tiny sketches of pots with inflated breads toppling over the edges line the cursive text, berries doodled in corners alongside ideas for how to achieve the perfect puff. I tend to turn to these for inspiration, and he's never seemed to mind, but it's been a while. Now, looking over them, I realize any of these sound better than this week's rustic English countryside inspired menu. My thoughts retreat to last weekend's workshop and Mika's creations. I don't have that level of creativity. Never been my strong suit. To make matters worse, I think I overused the word *fusion* too much when explaining my dishes. Anxiety grips me. The only reason I am a chef is because Mika and I went 50-50 with Aunt Jo's money on Iris. It was half-joke, half-strategy. If it was up to pure skill, I wouldn't be here. I'd be in the crew, if I was lucky. I rewrite the menu again and again until it looks more like his journals than my own. I text Mika the changes, telling him he should run the night's menu. He's up early because he replies with, "no final changes. Our menu is good."

*Our.*

I organize the office until there's nothing left to alphabetize.

That evening, the whole crew shows up confident and cleaned up. No hangovers detected. Lionel is baby-faced, for once, though the ever-present light snow of dandruff remains on his black jacket. Massie throws him a wink in admiration. She waltzes into the dining room carrying two plates: braised chutney lamb and a plate of squid ink risotto—a pile of black tar missing the artful green note of a basil leaf.

Eddie shakes his head in some kind of teenage agony, eyes glued to her ass.

*Basil. Basil. Basil. You idiot!*

I try to make it in time, but she's out the door.

*Zero days without a fucking mistake.*

I go back to cleaning off my Mac Mighty MTH 80 knife, slightly annoyed. The pockmarked handle slices the air with a flick of my wrist. My hands look like fleshy extensions, part of the same machine.

"You okay?" Mika whispers.

I'm distracted, trying to peer out at the dining room. Mika knows better than to take me out of my element. He stretches his arm onto the table, letting it fall on my wrist.

"Chef—sorry, but we need you to okay these dishes," Eddie says.

I throw Eddie a dazed look.

*Snap out of it. Focus.*

I pace toward the corner, trying to maintain my cool. Trying to catalog the hour's events.

Eddie places the dishes in front of me, perfectly presented. I lean in to smell the plum honey sauce glazing over the lamb. The meat sinks in a bed of whipped parsnips. Eddie raises a wooden spoon for me to taste. I let out a grateful grunt and lick the mixture off my lips. A triumphant medley of mushrooms and pepper. *Bliss.* Almost good enough to forget the basil incident. Almost.

The whole staff watches as the plate goes out.

"Alright, everyone. Back to work. This is just a normal Friday night and our customers expect our usual greatness. Hmm?"

We try our best to pretend, incredibly aware that across the room, the critic is seated at our singles table, along the burgundy leather wall.

A perfect poker face, she gives us no indication of how she feels. Her face reminds me of a cartoon mouse: little nose, little lips, and an old-fashioned bowl haircut framing yellow panes around two inkwells. There's no use in guessing. I retreat to the weeds, to get lost in the blur of critics inside my head. Process, details, memory.

An hour later, Marissa comes by my office to tell me the critic has left. My stomach twists in knots the rest of the night. Mika and a few other staff are discussing the night in hushed voices near closing time. They must be swapping worst-case scenario stories because the lot of them avert my gaze. Mika brushes them off. I return to my notes, aware he's coming towards me.

Two giant hands slam onto the countertop.

"I'm not interested in armchair psychics," I declare, unable to fool myself.

Mika slides his elbows across the travertine.

"Cut it out. I just cleaned that."

"You get annoyingly anal when you're stressed, you know." He sighs. "The crew thought she looked satisfied."

"God, I need a smoke if I have to hear the rest of this."

He chuckles and pats his breast pocket. Marlboro Reds.

When we step into the alleyway, I feel my cheeks redden in the cold. Mika lifts a bag of trash off the steps and dumps it into a nearby bin. He draws out a pack, pulls out a cig, and carries it to my lips. A lighter flicks and the temporary heat is satisfying against my face, especially in the bleak dark of the alley.

"So, what did they say?"

Mika's eyebrows arch into his temple wrinkles.

"Well—"

Then—

"Don't sugarcoat it, Mika. They're always playing it up with you."

Mika leans forward. The tips of his ears catch the light like PVC foil.

"Why do you say that?"

"You know perfectly well why." I blink. "They know you tell me things and it's an excuse for the hostesses to flirt with you."

I make note of the well-dressed, drunken apparitions across the street. Mika throws the cigarette butt on the wet concrete.

"They know I'm basically married."

"Exactly."

I take one last puff and let it seep out of the corner of my mouth. I like him like this. Without strings or walls, just Mika. It's almost enough to make me forget the critic, or why I care. The truth is I don't. At least, not in that way. I'm angry that the girl I used to be is getting in the way. I'm angry an *outsider* can tell I'm faking it: I wasn't born with *the gift; any gift*. There was no *a-ha!* moment in my childhood where I was prodigious at something or destined for greatness. No great sign I would write about in a memoir years from now. And because of that, there's no justice, no reason in my having survived.

Mika is looking at me like he can read all my thoughts. Like I am some perfectionist whose life's work depends on the vote of critics. It's the story he knows. It's not my story.

"Look. The food was impeccable tonight. I mean, Eddie! His distraction with the waitress didn't even have an effect on his ability to prepare a decent steak."

I relent with a nod, suspicious of his closeness. He's doing that thing men do when they're trying to soften the blow, avoiding my eyes.

"That critic is gonna write good things and you won't know what to do with yourself."

"A problem I'd like to have." I snort.

Mika squeezes my shoulders the way he used to do when we were together. I'm mid-memory when he comes around the table and spins me around to face him, holding me at an arm's length.

"Hey. Look at me." His voice is suddenly serious. "Jesus, your eyes are really red."

"Oh, yeah. It's nothing. I haven't been able to sleep lately. You know, the usual thing . . . "

My voice trails off, unsure of how much to share. Those secrets again. I pull away into the shadow, where the backlight doesn't reach.

"I'm taking care of it."

I can sense Mika contemplating my health in silence. But before he can say anything else, a woman rolls in on a Honda CB300². Mika shifts away, creating a bigger gap between us, so I immediately know it's Hannah. The headlights bounce off the wall, casting long shadows along the street. She uncorks her helmet, letting a long blonde ponytail fall to her back.

"Babe, you ready?"

Mika returns the wink, walking down and wrapping his arms around her waist. Hannah kisses him and hands him a spare helmet.

"Hey, Toni," she says, readjusting her jacket.

A couple of years ago, we were all having dinner at Mika's friends' restaurant, and Hannah and I were seated at the same table. We were discussing names and Hannah was tipsy.

"Antonia is so . . . gets stuck on the tongue. How about Toni?"

"Toni's Pizza? Toni's Deli? No, thank you."

Mika gives me a half-hearted, "See you tomorrow," and they ride off, leaving me in the dark. The motorcycle lights blur away into the wet pavement. A dark figure shuffles from the dumpster into the alley light, and I make out one of the lot's usual homeless people. He's an older man, with striking young eyes and a smile. Staring me down like he knows me. *You'd be the first*, I think.

I head on inside, locking the door behind me.

All the same, can't be too careful.

# ACT II

# **WORK HAPPENS.** Days go on.

You don't need to know about it because there's nothing to tell. Maybe I'm losing interest. Maybe I'm already editing what I want you to know.

I spend a whole day coming up with new dishes. My inspiration collage is laid out in old cookbooks and vintage prints on my computer. The result is a mismatched trail of desserts and entrees, technically perfect, but hollow. My journal is open on the counter, and it looks nothing like Mika's. There's no cohesion. No artful tact. Only scribbles and the recycled brain drain of everything I've ever read.

I leave the dishes there to rot, and change into the crewneck and jeans hanging in my office. The door clicks behind me and soon it's clear the night is too cold for what I'm wearing. The fabric raises around my stomach like a protruding tumor.

I stride along the wet street until I bump into a trail of warm bodies standing in line. A beautiful girl chatters away on the phone next to me. She's meeting someone here, keeps poking her head out of the line to look down the street. Every so often, she turns her head in my direction, waves of honey-blonde sticking to her lip gloss. The person on the other end is having trouble finding the place.

"*Fames*," she enunciates with an out-of-state accent.

Either she is mispronouncing it or I'm not *in the know*.

The line goes by slowly, so I'm casing the joint out where I can. Two exits, security guards, coat check. *Pixel had that, too*. The blood rushes to my head, intoxicating me with strange memories. *Grab onto the wall, Antonia*. The girl in front of me looks at me warily—probably thinks this is the face I make before I hurl. The pulsing under my feet feels promising. Promising because it's the only thing matching my heart palpitations.

There's a flash of someone's face from Pixel in the crowd and I am about to bolt when—

"Next!"

The night goblin is back. Inside, *Fames* is dark. Underworld dark. Fake Roman pillars painted red, green glow lights spread over the ceiling like varicose veins. The DJ is not playing EDM or Top-100 remixes. Instead, there's a discordant howling, alternative strings pulling on low E notes. Around me, bodies sway in synchronized patterns. The cave buzzes with insect-like vibrations. Goosebump-skinned dancers swirl into the middle of the room, where an emerald bar counter stands framed with potion bottles of booze in strange shapes and colors. A mix of Party City and gauche dinner party decor.

The girl from outside stretches out her hands beautifully on the dance floor. She looks like a statue of Demeter, wearing black jeans and a flowy white top. A brush of an indigo organza scarf around her neck. Her beauty is almost primal, otherworldly. The rest of the people watch as the melodic hum from the DJ's station pulses out. Then a crescendo of strings sends the lights flashing. Deep blue and white dots cover the ceiling. My mind goes blank. We all dance.

Spinning and spinning.

Spinning until I'm closer to her.

"You're so beautiful." My words are slurred.

She smiles at me and keeps dancing. For a moment, the light catches her hair in a memory. I'm back at Pixel, dancing in front of Alice. My chest heaves and there's a ringing in my ears. I push through the crowd and grip the edge of the bar. I'm sweating, with the familiar sensation of a kid who's gone too far into the deep end of the pool. I scan the club for the exit.

Too many people. I have to get out.

By the bar, a man watches me. Piercing blue eyes and

white hair like a flame on his head. Ears all pointed like an elf's. Even so, I would have missed him if he wasn't in the way. The air smells familiar, heavy with the reminder of a long night. Every muscle in my body screams to leave.

Avoiding further eye contact, I zipline to the exit and out into the night. There's a lick of cold sweat on the back of my neck—

And something else.

The feeling of being watched.

I'm too freaked out to walk any farther and end up taking an overpriced cab back to my apartment. I can't get Fames or that strange man out of my head. Unsure of what my gut is trying to tell me, I chalk it up to bad memories and sit in the shower until the hot water runs out. How long has it been since I slept? I rest my head against the shower wall and think about the double life created in my non-working hours. Maybe I should see someone. But who? *You can tell Mika.*

Once I'm out of the shower, I turn on the tv just to have noise in the apartment. I write everything down in my journal, to keep track. Either way, it's more interesting than my attempts at new recipes.

A week later, I still haven't slept. What's worse, there's a new buzzing that's taken up residence in my left ear. I touch the tip of my ears and a jolt of pain shudders through my neck. Over the sink, I lean in and let a steady drip of castor oil flood my ear. I've been in a mood since that night and trying to hide it from the others. The crew is already in the kitchen when I arrive. A bad sign. The pained quiet strikes me as soon as I open the door. They're circled around the counter space with a folded copy of today's newspaper, quickly folded as I enter my office. It doesn't matter. I already know what the headlines say:

*"Perfectly Fine food at Hip-Midtown Spot."*

# VALENTINA ROJAS

*"Technically exquisite."*

No mention of the poetry of my work. The poetry I've tried so desperately to fake. I'm angry and thinking about how we should have changed the menu for Mika's. Dinnertime goes by in a blur.

Time, for once, speeds up.

It's a different crowd tonight at Fames.

I keep waiting for the music to hit: to hypnotize my body out of myself. All of my attempts to make a new life have failed. And these memories of that night keep coming back, whispering tales of the trauma which has never felt mine. As if on cue, the eerie melody lifts my thoughts. I dance for a good fifteen minutes. It's an innate sort of music: my body knows how to move, like I've rehearsed the beats and drops in my dreams.

Suddenly, a sound goes off. Rapid fireworks in the sky above us. My body drops to the ground. My head is full of thunder.

*Don't do it. Don't do it. Not here.*

Around me, hungry eyes watch with a mix of curiosity and worry. Two bouncers crowd a young man in the middle of the dance floor. The main suspect, I think. But I don't stay to find out. I hold my breath and race to the exit.

Outside, the pulsing has resumed. Like nothing happened.

"Here, breathe, breathe."

A stranger is holding my hands.

It's the man with the elfish face from last week. The dark elf.

"I'm okay. I'm okay," I reply, tersely.

"I was wondering when you'd break down, to be honest. Surprised it took you this long."

I rise to my feet.

"Excuse me?"

Then—

"Are you watching me?"

But I already know the answer.

"Not on purpose. My work takes me all over. I think I've seen you at every club I've been to. Don't you ever sleep?"

A pause.

"Hey, it's my business to notice. That's not a crime, now is it?"

I have to concede that. I take his hand. My feet feel like I'm still dancing.

Once we are both eye-level, he hands me a cigarette and lights one up for himself. Normally, I would be suspicious of a stranger like this—aren't all serial killers totally charming? But that old gut feeling isn't kicking in, whether because of my imagined near-death experience or sleep deprivation. I inhale and let the smoke sit on my tongue a bit, eyes closed. My body shifts a little. The man leans me back up. His hands are warm, familiar.

"Think if I'm preventing you from fainting, you should know—the name is Booth."

"Booth?" I want to say something witty but, Swiss cheese.

"So what is your poison?"

"Excuse me?"

"Well, pardon me, miss, but no well-adjusted—" He squints his eyes and pushes a coil out of my face. "—thirty-something is out in clubs like this one at 3 am."

"Pretty judgmental for another thirty-something to say."

A snort from him. A pause.

"My poison is sleep. That is what I want. Don't suppose you have that in a bottle."

"Come on."

I stare at his figure as it moves away from me, wondering if any of this is real. It's hard to let go of that trance of almost-sleep and the thought of its full potential being within my grasp is tantalizing. Does Alice follow the

White Rabbit? Booth exhales, a plume sighing out of him. He turns and raises his eyebrows.

"Well?"

It often happens in cities that friendships are created out of thin air. Chance encounters on the subway, or shared accidents. Booth leads me by the arm all the way to the subway, then two blocks or so to a quiet neighborhood. A stark white, Malibu-esque high rise bulges off the corner street. The safe part of town, he states, as if this will keep me going. We reach a small archway with a well-lit path, a garden laid out beyond its gates, leading to a modern glass door.

"This is me."

He throws me a knowing look.

"Come on then. You can barely stand."

The night goblin leads me through. He doesn't feel unsafe, though it's hard to tell. We enter the well-lit lobby, which has a valet. A couple of neighbors walk past us, as if they can't tell we're here. I manage a cough, just to try something. Lean my body in, so they can smell me. Bleach, fry grease, smoke. There's two of them congregating towards the door, close to feel the chill of the air seeping through the door creases. Nothing. The elevator's tired groan alerts them to our presence, but they hardly look back, even as Booth and I get sucked in to the small square space, a greenish light rendering us pale and nightmarish. One of them makes a face at something outside and the woman laughs, a pearly sound of joy hitching itself to the walls of the elevator, keeping us company all the way up.

The inside of his apartment is eclectic beyond measure. I can't help but marvel at the assortment of trinkets—tiny Peruvian dolls, Lisa Frank folders framed on the wall, pillows in the shape of amused looking ghosts, and a metal wall covered in strange magnets. A slew of 3D art pieces hangs like skin-tags off the brightly colored turquoise wall. Seashells disguised as bowls fill the air with their rich incense. The walls are covered in a paisley pink wallpaper that sheens with the glow of the pre-dawn light, streaming in from the three-paned windows behind. I've time-traveled but am confused which era. There's something familiar about it.

"Welcome to Casa de Booth."

Booth waves towards the white, leather couch by the windows, tightening his robe. I can't remember if he was always wearing that. He leads me to a room off the hallway, and drags a bunch of blankets off the shelf. There's a strange diffuser in each room emitting a wonderful smelling mist—my eyes droop as his figure moves towards a large chest and pulls out a bag.

"Don't worry. I'm not going to try anything. In fact, I have to go. Stay here until you feel better, okay?"

He shuts the door quietly and I'm alone.

It crosses my mind that I should have just gone home. I snap out of it and sit on the guest bed, listening. When I know he's gone for sure, I poke my head out and walk around the apartment. It's strange to get to know someone's space intimately before you know them. Outside, the city blurs in a carpet of rain. Where could he possibly be going at this time of night?

I cross the living room to where one of the diffusers sits: a typical looking small vase with a hole at the top. Reminds me of those picture books about small whales and kid explorers. As if on cue, the sound of the mist spritzing into the air wheezes out. My muscles loosen, nostrils flare, arms feel leaden. The weight of sleep lures me back onto the bed, in spite of my curiosity. The bed is particular—rounded and encased in a periwinkle, suede bed frame. A particular frame for a particular man. It's cloaked in velvet cushions, inviting me to jump in. Wee! My body sinks in like it's a cloud. The diffuser exhales again. My eyelids droop. I sink into the pillow. It smells like vanilla and pine. How long had it been?

For normal people, sleep is often the solution to terrible nights. Sleep off the guilt, the drunkenness, the pain. Sleep off the victimhood of the day. I manage to open my eyes once more to scan the room, then follow the velvet dreamscape to my own hands. Little rashes have broken out near the smeared stamp from the club and I'm trying not to scratch. The apartment walls are closing in. I shut my eyes and let go.

It's seven when I wake up again. The rain outside has stopped and I feel a maddening urge to leave. The whole place is too quiet for my liking.

Booth never shows. There's a note on the door with his cell.

"Call me next time you can't sleep."

Days pass without a break.

I keep waiting for the night when my body finally gives in, but it doesn't come. Instead, the mind goes. Decaying thoughts that bruise into unspoken darkness.

Mika has taken a few days off at Iris and I welcome the extra work. Keeps me structured throughout the waking hours. Under my nostrils is the memory of Booth's place. I keep wondering if I will run into him, daydreaming about returning to that warm bed. A strange thought. A 3 AM thought creeping into the sobering daylight.

At night, however, when the rooms are quiet and Iris is empty, my thoughts return to Booth and that strange apartment.

## When did you know

Booth leaves my message on Read all evening. It isn't until midnight when I finally get a reply back.

## Come to my place and I'll show you

I walk back and forth in my room until I finally can't stand it any longer. Outside my apartment, the stairwell is brilliantly cold. The small windowsill overlooking the basketball court looks like a dark portal to the other world. There's bird shit there, too, I think, noting the wet trails of white lines dripping into the corners. I can't see much of anything past the shadows except a figure making its way to the subway, in a hurry. Perhaps the other me is also running away from something.

A thick blanket of smoke greets me when the doors open, though I am unsure who has opened the door. There's a murmur of conversation, jovial laughter ringing from every corner of Booth's apartment—teeming with all manner of people. I've been in the city long enough to pick them out as artists, daytime psychics maybe, trust fund black sheep, models. A woman with two hoop earrings, a rhinestone tiger cradled in both arches, hands me a flute of champagne. I take it while beaming back at her toothy smile like a total deer in the headlights.

"Antonia! There you are, you sly minx." Booth waves me in like an old friend, someone who is as familiar with every pocket of his nature as he is the space he occupies. He's more ordinary than I remember him, though that could just be the utter eccentricity of his other guests.

"You made it."

He leads me through the kitchen where I spot a few magnets, moved around since last I was here. There's a rough tree made out of State magnets, and clouds from plain business card stickers. It looks positively mundane next to the bead curtain overhead. There are used Turkish coffee cups, intricate and small, in the bottom of a farmhouse sink. Plastered along the wall are vintage black and whites, family trees in some, ghostly-blue eyes in others.

"I collect those. Do you like them?"

He's caught me looking around, and it seems like this is part of going down the hole to wonderland.

"And that—Don't you like that? Something else more your speed?"

A man laughs behind him. I gulp the champagne down.

Tickles in the back of my mouth. There is one thing missing. The diffuser! The place smells unfamiliar.

We pass through to the other side of the heavy bead curtain and end up in the living room, facing a circle of people dangling around a velvet couch.

Booth takes my hand and slumps into the corner loveseat, next to a woman with honey-colored hair wearing a periwinkle, babydoll 1960s frock. One look at those dark brown eyes and I am teleported back to the very first night at Fames. *Demeter*.

"You've met Aurelia."

"Enchanting!" she exclaims with an accented-English. Laughter from all around us. Booth pats her on the thigh as if to indicate the charm of her misnomer for the correct reply.

"Ah," Booth says. "This is the beautiful Diane. Diane, meet Toni."

Before I can protest, Diane reaches over Booth and leans in with her incredibly long neck. She kisses me on each cheek and yanks me down next to her. I nearly take down both Booth and Aurelia. The spot on the couch is warm and sunken in.

"Booth always brings the tastiest of friends."

"I bet," I say, finally finding my voice.

The bubbly has hit the bottom of my empty stomach.

"But what are the rules?"

"Rules?" Booth's face is amused, eyebrows lifting into his hairline.

"Every group has rules. You're nightowls, evidently. You all like to dance . . . and what else?"

"Only one rule, darling—we don't want anyone conventional here." Diane says, dragging a cigarette between her lips.

A man with midnight skin shakes his hands, dangling with bracelets, at another dressed in all wool. The two exchange a bit of banter which I can't follow, and the group erupts into laughter.

# A FEAST OF PUTRID DELIGHTS

Booth jumps out of his seat and disappears for a few minutes. In his absence, Diane commandeers the conversation, and starts recounting a hunting tale which sounds like something out of the 19th century. The faces I have not been introduced to sit and listen, nodding at times, sipping away at pink flutes of clear liquor. No one asks me the usual questions—*where are you from? what do you do? what part of the city are you from?* They seem neutrally indifferent. No supplicants to social norms or manners. It's both freeing and terrifying. How does one act? *Unconventional*, I suppose.

Booth returns, carrying more champagne for the table. He claps his hands and a barstool with velvet cushions appears, handed to him by one of the men dressed in wool tuxes. The lot of them roar with applause, as if this is a magnificent undertaking.

"You're still here."

"What kind of question is that?"

"Nothing. Just wasn't sure. Thought we'd scared you off." Diane drops to her knees and pantomimes an aerobic dancer staring up at the ceiling while her hands grab one of the flutes.

"Shall we begin?"

The crowd cheers.

Then—

Booth scoots forward, the redistributed weight sinking me into my seat. Annoyed, I lean in. Whatever it is, I'm game. The cart juts open, revealing a dandelion wisp on a spinner. The drug is spooled from the stem, like a shrunken cotton candy, and passed around. They all pull a wisp and place it on their tongues. Diane takes hers, gives me a wink, and closes her eyes. Moments later, tears stream down her perfect foundation. Her mouth hangs open, tongue dropping out like a rose petal.

The people around me look high in a very different way than what I'm used to. They're in control of their bodies, instead of lethargic creatures with no motivation, or hyperactive artists. Alert and sure of themselves, they sit upright, devoid of all inebriation; a woman in a low ponytail, crowned with jewels, sinks into a corner chair, unveils an easel and colorful paints, and starts stroking the canvas. The man with golden bangles starts to sing, his melodic opera filling the room with agonizing sorrow.

"To the sleepless!"

They toast glasses of champagne and fall into disparate conversations. Booth slumps beside me with yet another champagne flute offering.

"The who?"

Booth glances around the room, as if my questions bore him.

"I couldn't hold down a job before. Now look."

"At what? Your lucrative drug business?"

"Tsk, I'm spreading the gospel."

"You sure it's not adrenaline?"

"I'm perfectly calm, in case you can't see it. There may not be a cure to insomnia but ah, look at them. Beautiful creatures."

We sit silently for a couple moments, watching them. Booth gestures to one of the guests and says to me, "See her. The one with the ponytail. That's Liv. She used to be real messed up. Daddy issues, history of abuse. The like. Took Cloud. Now she's a sought-after tattoo artist."

"How does it work?" I ask, playing into it.

"You've heard that mushrooms change you, right? Give you clarity and all that bullshit. Well, this is nothing compared to that. This is *real* clarity."

"What are you really after then, money?"

"Ouch, Toni."

"Well–"

"We have a non-believer in our midst!"

My eyes bug at the pastel wisp in his hand. I almost reach for it. But I have more questions.

Sure, around me, fantastic artists and creators were

engaged in new conversations. Not any of that recycled shit. They had meaning. Yet—

"I think if someone tells you they've found the meaning of life, the answer, you should keep one hand on your wallet and keep walking."

"Maybe so. But everyone here has been invited."

"You said it works like that for everyone?"

"Pretty much."

"I took it once, you know."

He laughs and slams the drink on the table.

"Not possible. You must have taken the early batches. They weren't this magnus opus . . . "

"How would you know?"

"Well, what happened?"

"I fell asleep. I was out for days."

"Hmm."

"Last time, too—"

I lean in to sniff it. Vanilla. Pine.

"It's in the diffusers, no?"

He shrugs.

"Sometimes. Call it microdosing."

"I slept, too. I never sleep."

"Maybe that's your talent, Toni. You're good at sleeping."

I couldn't recall the last time my memory is this good. Or when the exhaustion isn't keeping me from feeling like a fumigated bug. I am exhausted daily, unable to do anything extraordinary. Every muscle in my body craves relief. And here is something good that could come out of it. Maybe I am just looking a gift horse in the mouth, or however that ridiculous saying goes. Maybe sleep is exactly what I need.

Shadows and teeth smile all around me, and though any other day this would have seemed unsettling, I take them as an invitation.

Booth holds the Cloud between his fingers casually, like this is no big deal. I accept it.

Between my fingers, it's thicker than it looks.

Cotton candy. Stuff of childhoods.

I open my mouth and place it there, on my tongue, letting it dissolve with my saliva. Tastes like nothing at all. Nothing of consequence.

"There's a catch, though."

*What the fuck, Booth*.

He *tsks* my outrage away.

"Nothing like that. It's just, well, you're one of us now. You're gonna see the world differently. You're gonna see it as it is."

Before he turns away from me, he slips a pocketful of Cloud in my jacket.

"For later."

Booth gets up and the couch exhales a pleathered squeak. Diane has gone over to admire the painter's work. Someone is dancing with Aurelia. We're all still listening to the man's voice fill the space, a fever dream with no end in sight.

The time passes by in creative successes. There is a playwright in the corner who has been talking off the wall about characters, and now has completed Act I of their play. Aurelia has taken the lead, and they perform it in front of us: a comedy about the end of water, and alien mermaids who come up with the brilliant idea to start a new Wall Street in the middle of the Pacific Ocean. Weird as it sounds, I enjoy the monologue of the human protagonist, who has, of course, fallen in love with one of the Merpeople. By the time I check the time, a red dawn light is creeping into the flat. I don't feel any different. Booth has disappeared again, so I say goodbye to Diane, kiss Aurelia good night, and walk back home.

My ears are still throbbing by the time I get home. Nothing feels different. I sit in front of the tv, thinking every new feeling is going to be The Feeling. Maybe it was some sort of communal delusion. Maybe he didn't even give me the real thing. I fall into bed and curl up under the covers. Outside, the commotion of cars and city life blares on. Before I can curse his name, I fall asleep.

Booth has opened a door.

I wake up feeling incredible. What's more, I wake up at *noon*. When I check my phone, I realize it's Monday. I've slept for two days straight.

I'm no Sleeping Beauty when I wake up, of course. There's a light rash on my ass from where I have soiled myself. The first thing I feel is the rot furring at my teeth. I hack myself into the shower, trying to quiet the memory of day-old urine. I flick the earwax built up into the drain and brush my teeth vigorously. At least the taste of mint pushes by my hunger headache. I'm famished. My stomach growls the moment I gain consciousness in the waking world. Slipping out of the shower, I scour my fridge, naked, full of homemade stocks and salsa, and pluck out a jar of Mika's peach jam. I pop two pieces of bread into the toaster and am immediately overwhelmed by a gagging sensation. Instead of sweetness, it feels like I've eaten the bottom of a fridge's slime. When I open the jar, a wave of nausea and disgust hits me. The smell is egregious—dirty belly button mixed with puke. I can't decide which is worse but both at once is an assault on my nostrils. Feels like I'm a lopsided balloon in need of a bucket, quick. Has the jar gone bad? I check the date. Best by—All good there. Or maybe? I zip into my room to pick up my phone, almost taking a tumble. That's another thing. The memory of getting up comes back to me in bursts, like a puzzle that isn't all there. Legs buzzing with sleep, the painful walk (crawl) to the bathroom.

Side effects. *There are bound to be side effects, Antonia*. It doesn't matter. It's worth it. I get dressed and leave without eating.

I walk down the street feeling like everything's entirely new. Every step is light—I glide down the pavement, threading through the people as if I am made of air. Soup,

soup! We are nothing but soup, fragments of vittles floating through the miasma of broth and steel! There are a dozen pairs of eyes with an appalled side eye (no one in the city would allot for more than that) but they're all distorted to me, unable to keep me from flying through. If I had known, I would have taken Cloud the first night I met Booth. I would have thrown it all away. There's no trace of brain fog or wooziness for the first time in years. I can only try to erase all evidence of that stench waiting for me in my apartment. Almost.

I emerge out of the subway and head straight towards Iris. The white sun slants through the bloated skyline and leaves the pedestrians covered in cool, long shadows. There are strange things happening, sure, but nothing to be alarmed about.

My eyes focus. I am a camera. Whirring in. The figures materialize. There's a kid staring up at me at the stoplight, eating a cereal bar. At least, that is what it looks like. What it smells like is another story entirely. It's rank, wet dog mixed with a metallic tinge. I think I am going to hurl right here in the street. The light turns green. My walking slows. Now there is a woman sipping a coffee—coffee with notes of old eggs and body odor. The unpleasant city smells are turned up to full blast under my nose.

Except those things.

When I get to work, Mika and the crew are prepping dinner, testing out a few dishes. I cross the kitchen and realize the food wobbling around on the porcelain does *not* look delicious. It's off-color, for one: rancid, gray, slimy. An acid trip vision of decaying seafood. Was it always jello? I blink and nothing happens. The vision stays the same.

I know the dish is supposed to be steak but all I see is a heap of gray, like a shrunken whale with a wound of green fungus split across the middle. Hard to say, really. My mind is playing tricks on me. I'm hungry and nauseated.

I hold onto the counter, trying my best not to hurl,

when a Kirby tattoo appears in front of me, smack dab on Eddie's left shoulder.

"Something wrong, Chef?" Eddie asks.

*Your chef is having a bad trip. Wouldn't be the first.*

"No, Eddie, I'm fine. Go ahead."

Another plate, equally as disgusting, passes by.

"Is that dish really going out that way?"

I cusp my hand over my mouth. The smell is unbearable: rotten eggs again, swimming in stale air.

"Look, boss. If you're sick, you really shouldn't be here . . ."

I shake my head.

"Bring that back."

They stare at me like I'm losing it. Mika's head pokes up.

"No, Chef. The meat is fresh. It's Butcher Ale's."

"What is it, Antonia? Are you okay?"

"Nothing, it's fine. I just had a question about the dish. No big deal."

"She said it smelled rancid, but it's not . . ."

*Tattletale.*

"Maybe Chef is pregnant," Massie sneers.

I turn away and head towards my office, playing it off. It's hard enough to hold my breath and keep from smelling the food.

Mika knocks.

"I just have a migraine. I'm okay."

*Just go away.*

Mika knocks again.

"I'm fine, Mika, really."

The image of the slimy globs won't stop replaying in my mind. My clothes, hair—it all smells foul. I run over to my desk and pull out the trash can, feeling it fuzzing at my teeth. I hurl.

For the rest of the evening, I lie down in the dark, blinds shut, door closed. On the other side, I can hear the end-of-day commotion. After a few minutes of vacuuming, the kitchen falls quiet.

Mika knocks again but this time, he doesn't wait for a response. He slumps into the doorway, adjusting his scarf.

"You're alive."

"Yeah."

"You should really try not to push yourself if you're sick."

I want to find Booth and kill him.

"I'm up. Let's go."

We step out into the alley, where the rest of the crew waits, avoiding my gaze. Amir, the pâtissier, drags his cigarette, taking in a huge puff. Massie's got her hands in her pockets, flirting with Eddie a few steps over.

"You want to come join us, Chef? We're all going to Blind Tiger to get hammered and eat," Amir says. He must have gotten here late.

"Yeah, I'm starving."

"Do you think that's a good idea?" Mika whispers.

"Whoa, I think Chef can handle a few beers—once she's had some bread, of course," Eddie jokes. *Right, of course he thinks it's a hangover. Better than a pregnancy.*

"I'm alright now, and besides, the tank is empty."

Mika looks unconvinced. We head down the street, and I start to feel okay. This is a good idea, I tell myself. I have to eat, bad trip or not.

When we get to Blind Tiger, all of the service world is crammed at the bar. Several hostesses scamper out of the kitchen with plastic bins of fried food. A dark-haired bartender I don't recognize is behind the bar, patiently listening to each patron's order over the music. Mika and Amir are the first to snake through successfully, and call us over to a table, which is still being cleaned up by a short-haired, petite woman. She wipes the bumpy wood surface over with a wet rag and brings us a couple of menus. I'm already sitting down, bunching up my coat under my seat, when Massie slips a laminated one-page menu into my hand. A whiff of fried food infiltrates my nostrils and I try not to gag.

# A FEAST OF PUTRID DELIGHTS

The waitress swings by with our pickles and an extra order of cheese fries. "On the house," she says, winking at Amir. Mika makes a suggestive face and they all dig in. Instead of salty goodness, the stench of putrefied seafood wafts up my nose. *Not again.* I start to sweat, full of nausea. The stink is oozing out of my pores. My eyes land on the last basket of pickles. In the plastic bin, the rank miasma of the ocean swims around in a brown oil, bubbling with a shimmering film.

By now, it's been a full 48 hours since I last ate. I don't know whether to barf or gag, and unsure of what will come out of my mouth next, I make a beeline for the bathroom. It's single and occupied. Opposite the women's bathroom door, two clean-shaven men hang on one another, swaying.

"Can't believe you made me do that extra shot."

"Fuck, I didn't make you do anything."

Impatiently, the shorter one bangs on the door.

"Take a shit at home. Hurry up."

Within seconds, a flustered man emerges from the bathroom. The two men bust in, making crude comments about the odor. The last thing I see before the door closes is one of them unzipping over the sink, his face flushed with relief.

It's too late. I throw up before I can make it to the restroom catching the mealy chunks with my hands. When the door opens, I hear a woman groan in disgust at the smell and I slip in to clean myself off.

"Great timing," I hiss.

I return to the table smelling like antibacterial soap.

"Jesus. What's wrong with you?" Massie yells over the table.

I wave her away.

"Your cell, Mika. Give me your cell."

"Uh, yeah sure—"

There's a new level of fear in his voice, like he thinks I'm finally going to call Hannah and confess everything, years later.

Mika follows me outside.

"Booth?"

I try to walk into the corner so Mika doesn't hear me.

"Do you need another round already?" Booth's voice sounds particularly static on the other end of the phone.

"Listen to me. This shit is laced or something. It's been like two days and I'm hallucinating. I can't even—"

"Hold up. I don't dabble in that kind of drug dealing. Cloud is special and I only give to a very select group of people. I told you."

I'm already annoyed with his flair for self-indulgence.

"I am really messed up here."

There's a pause.

"I never heard of someone getting tripped up on this stuff. Are you sick or something?"

"I'm as healthy as a horse."

"Listen, I'm sorry, this isn't on me, kid. You just gotta sweat it out."

"I slept. For two days. Is that normal?"

"Slept? No one sleeps. There's no cure . . . "

"Well. I did. I told you. I asked you—"

"Nothing else?"

I think of the woman in a ponytail painting a galaxy sky.

"No."

Another pause.

"Huh. Maybe sleeping is your skill, like I said."

"Booth—"

He cuts me off mid-protest.

"I gotta go, Toni. Call me back later."

So much for friendship. The last comment feels like a punch in the gut. I breathe in sharply. *Sweat it out.* All I've done since the kitchen is sweat it out. My stomach grumbles.

"Here."

I hand Mika back his cell, which pings with three unread messages from Hannah.

"What was that?"

"Side effects from my new meds."

"You have your doctor's cell memorized?"

"Yeah, he's cool."

He gives me a look.

"It's the food. It disgusts me. I can't look at it."

I stare at my feet.

"What's wrong?"

"I guess I haven't eaten."

"Look. I know I can't fix whatever this side effect is, but the hungry thing, I can fix."

"What do you mean?"

"Remember when your parents died, and you couldn't eat at all and you got so skinny?"

I hesitate for a moment; drink and chew. What else is there to do?

Moments later, we are back inside. Mika orders all of us a round of shots. The kind of tequila that burns going down.

I slam down the first two. The alcohol looks gray and cloudy and tastes like crud, but it's less horrific than the food. Mika pushes a plate of sliders my way, urging me to swallow them in large bites.

I swallow the first patty, trying not to retch. I wash it down with a large beer. Disgusting.

Some hours later, Mika is holding back my hair over my toilet.

"I guess we overdid it."

"The double sliders were a mistake—"

I shudder at the thought of them. The stink is all over my fingers. I'm cut off by another wave of vomit, though it's just water and spit at this point.

"At least you got the calorie intake."

"Shut up."

Mika chuckles, not taking his hand off my sweaty back. I wipe my mouth with a towel and sit up, head over to the sink, and gargle a shit ton of mouthwash.

Mika changes me out of my old shirt and into an oversized tee, like I'm a helpless kid. Nevertheless, a rush of emotion comes over me. I try to tell myself it's the nausea. We're still holding each other's gaze when the phone rings.

"Hey, baby. Yeah, I was just dropping off the guys. Designated sheepherder again. Yeah, just helping Antonia to her door. Okay. Love you, bye."

I stand over the sink again. Nausea or jealously?

"Hannah?"

He replies with a small, 'yes'. It's a stupid thing to ask, but it's good for creating distance.

"I should get going."

I wobble over to the door, telling him I'll be okay. When he leaves, I drag myself into bed, chucking the Cloud into the wastebasket beside my door.

Enough of that.

I'll be okay.

After a week, I think the hallucinations will go away.

Each day, I pop egg rolls or pizza bites into the oven. I follow bites of food with a shot of Skol vodka, or whatever I have on hand. Small things. Anything too large starts to resemble *The Thing*.

Work gets harder and harder. And the crew has begun to comment on it. No more jokes about pregnancy or hangover. No more slaps on the back. A hangover in our field of work is normal, expected. It's a skill every chef is seemingly born with. My own skill is working against me, because the crew knows I can hold my liquor. I can hold my own.

I see them whispering in corners. See them pulling Mika aside. What are they planning? Has the mutiny begun? Throughout the week, they bring out the tastiest dishes for the next few days for our usual testing. This is the hardest part: instead of subsiding, the Cloud side effects have increased.

# A FEAST OF PUTRID DELIGHTS

I'm in a world of hallucinations. Illusions of what the dish is and what it becomes happens all at once. A well-plated, meticulously designed plate of cod eggs and braised leeks shapeshifts into the decay of the ocean floor, the putrid insides of a neighbor cat, left unburied. And before all this, the *smells*. Weeks old grease build up emanating from a filo pastry, sitting atop the counter; the damp heat of armpits mixed with rust and fish food. Is this what Booth meant by the truth? Then it isn't so funny anymore. Maybe it never was.

The best I can do is split the work with Mika, come in three times a week and leave the rest to him. I feel bad because I know he's got Hannah and the baby on his mind. Then again, maybe I don't. After all, this was his dream first. Leaving me to carry the load was never the agreement. My whole reason for doing this was the promise of us. Not them.

My skin starts to break out. Lower chin and back mapped out like an elementary school pepperoni pizza. Boils with no exit holes pop up beneath my nose, hurtful to the touch. Cover up makes it worse, and no amount of water drinking fixes this fact. I'm seventeen again: lost, uncomfortable, tired. Frequent showering fails to erase the smell of throw-up. What's worse, my throat burns like it's on fire. I look up ED tips on Reddit on how to get rid of the sensation. Girls with usernames like "LolitaNervosa" and "BoollimaBetch" advise chewing bread then spitting it out, gargling milk. "Whatever you do, do not swallow!" So many jokes, so little will to type them up. Rubbing toothpaste around the gums seems to be the most agreed upon, less egregious take, so I pop into the convenience store near work and grab a travel-size tube. The following Wednesday, I finally call in sick. Mika sounds almost relieved over the phone.

With nothing left to do, I spend an hour in the bathroom, picking at my skin, compulsively inspecting every pore and grease build-up while a reality show blares in the background. The skin picking feels good in my soul and takes my mind off the hunger. The downside is it leaves my skin all red and puffy. A couple of exit wounds are leaking clear discharge and blood. I turn off all the main lights to avoid scaring myself.

A ribbon of oily hair bends off the side of my hair, made worse with the weight of my bun. I should shower but I'm too tired. Instead, I plop down on the sofa, rotting there for hours. The reality shows have gone from fashion-forward polygamist families to New York Real Estate talking heads with very big teeth, back to polygamists (more frumpy). When my butt gets too uncomfortable, I rise to retrieve more blankets. Only then do I notice how loosely my sweats fit, how I can feel the bony parts of my hips when I sit crisscrossed. I go into the storage closet—a functionless boiler room with one shelf—and drag out a dusty scale. Present from the aunt and her "what every woman needs" motto. The number on the scale is dipping below average, according to an internet search. But I don't believe it. Not yet. I head over to the cheap mirror hanging in my bathroom and promptly undress. Toes curling on the russet-colored linoleum floor. Eyes narrowing. My ass is flat, but it's never been super round. Gaze migrates over to my shoulders (yes, clavicle is present), then legs, then stomach. I suppose that is where you can tell the most. I no longer look "well-fed", like a 1950s card about drinking milk. Any peachiness in my skin has taken on a pallid look. The constellations of my freckles on my chest are faded. I look like the number on the scale. I can feel my bones adjust for a moment, visualizing them shifting under the warm blanket of skin. Well, I think irritably, I guess this is a real problem. I stand there, naked for a while, examining the strange new hair growths over my cunt, the blondish-brown hairs on my arms. They're coarser than I remember. The haphazard beginnings of a new coat. *Organic*. I do what any sensible person in my condition does: I scour the internet. I find a group of people who've lost their taste buds and start to write down tips: full calorie smoothies, nose plugs. As to the sight of food, there's nothing to do but close my eyes. I take notes on potential recipes, save the rest. The growling in my stomach is on the precipice of animal-growling intensity.

Booth has been ignoring my calls all week. He's receded to some figment of my imagination. One evening, I get a weird text from his assistant claiming he's in Spain. I didn't even realize he had an assistant. I used the last of my Cloud to sleep a week off, and now I am wide awake—hormones, hunger, and anger radiating throughout my body. No sleep and no eating. I wonder how long until my body gives out.

Luckily, the city doesn't sleep. I resume my goblin nights—only this time, I'm too tired to go inside. Mostly, I sit outside clubs and watch people go in and out, making sure there's no one suspicious around. I admit the paranoia has grown in the past few days. I see those faces from Pixel wherever I turn. Other times, I imagine a younger Mika shaking his head at me, crossing the street to go over to Hannah. In my most desperate moments, I see the bomber, his face obscured by the same decay overtaking every plate of food. He's within reach, and then disappears into a throng of passersby.

On a grim, wet and snowy evening, a man tosses me a pack of cigarettes and a tenner. He mentions he's seen me for a couple of days and wanted to help out.

"It's tough out here for the homeless."

I nod gently and make a decision to never return.

In my dream, I can eat again.

I'm at a diner, like the one I used to frequent downtown. The type you'd find in Indianapolis or Des Moines. Brown and dimly lit, with wooden booths and green pillows. From where I'm sitting, there's a standing tray with a steaming plate of General Tso's Chicken: the myth, the legend. Tumorous nuggets glazed in the cum of mediocrity. The plate resembles a heap of thick little fetuses. I won't insult it by calling it Chinese food, even in my dreams, but it's like mac & cheese to me, a category on its own. Many a frozen variety has passed through my gullet in the middle of the night, along with two or more shots of Glenfiddich. No one looking, granny undies on, belly out. None compares to how this must taste.

The waitress brings the plate over to me without saying a word. She's a pretty teen, a mishmash of the last decades' childhood stars and Diane. *Ah, Diane.* The forward beauty from Booth's group of eclectic friends, in a much grayer timeline. A garnish of basil rests on top of the glazed meat. Strange.

The waitress hands me a fork then recedes into the shadows. I'm aware she's on the sidelines watching, but I don't care. The warm paste latches onto the roof of my mouth. I let in a spoonful of white rice. I can't stop.

Don't stop eating. Don't stop eating. Don't stop eating. Don't stop eating. Don't stop eating. Don't stop eating. Don't stop eating. Don't stop eating. Don't stop eating. Don't stop eating. Don't stop eating. Don't stop eating. Don't stop eating. Don't stop eating. Don't stop eating. Don't stop eating. Don't stop eating. Don't stop eating. Don't stop eating. Don't stop eating. Don't stop eating. Don't stop eating. Don't stop eating. Don't stop eating. Don't stop eating. Don't stop eating. Don't stop eating. Don't stop eating. Don't stop eating. Don't stop eating. Don't stop eating. Don't stop eating. Don't stop eating. Don't stop eating. Don't stop eating. Don't stop eating. Don't stop eating. Don't stop eating. Don't stop eating. Don't stop eating. Don't stop eating. Don't stop eating. Don't stop eating. Don't stop eating. Don't stop eating. Don't stop eating. Don't stop eating. Don't stop eating. Don't stop eating. Don't stop eating. Don't stop eating. Don't stop eating. Don't stop eating. Don't stop eating. Don't stop eating. Don't stop eating. Don't stop eating. Don't stop eating. Don't stop eating. Don't stop eating. Don't stop eating. Don't stop eating. Don't stop eating. Don't stop eating. Don't stop eating. Don't stop eating. Don't stop eating. Don't stop eating. Don't stop eating.

Don't stop eating. Don't stop eating. Don't stop eating.
Don't stop eating. Don't stop eating. Don't stop eating.
Don't stop eating. Don't stop eating. Don't stop eating.
Don't stop eating. Don't stop eating. Don't stop eating.
Don't stop eating. Don't stop eating. Don't stop eating.
Don't stop eating. Don't stop eating. Don't stop eating.
Don't stop eating. Don't stop eating. Don't stop eating.
Don't stop eating. Don't stop eating. Don't stop eating.
Don't stop eating. Don't stop eating. Don't stop eating.
Don't stop eating. Don't stop eating. Don't stop eating.
Don't stop eating. Don't stop eating. Don't stop eating.
Don't stop eating. Don't stop eating. Don't stop eating.
Don't stop eating. Don't stop eating. Don't stop eating.
Don't stop eating. Don't stop eating. Don't stop eating.
Don't stop eating. Don't stop eating. Don't stop eating.
Don't stop eating. Don't stop eating. Don't stop eating.
Don't stop eating. Don't stop eating. Don't stop eating.
Don't stop eating. Don't stop eating. Don't stop eating.
Don't stop eating. Don't stop eating. Don't stop eating.
Don't stop eating. Don't stop eating. Don't stop eating.
Don't stop eating. Don't stop eating. Don't stop eating.
Don't stop eating. Don't stop eating. Don't stop eating.
Don't stop eating. Don't stop eating. Don't stop eating.
Don't stop eating. Don't stop eating. Don't stop eating.
Don't stop eating. Don't stop eating. Don't stop eating.
Don't stop eating. Don't stop eating. Don't stop eating.
Don't stop eating. Don't stop eating. Don't stop eating.
Don't stop eating. Don't stop eating. Don't stop eating.
Don't stop eating. Don't stop eating. Don't stop eating.
Don't stop eating. Don't stop eating. Don't stop eating.
Don't stop eating. Don't stop eating. Don't stop eating.
Don't stop eating. Don't stop eating. Don't stop eating.
Don't stop eating. Don't stop eating. Don't stop eating.
Don't stop eating. Don't stop eating. Don't stop eating.
Don't stop eating. Don't stop eating. Don't stop eating.
Don't stop eating. Don't stop eating. Don't stop eating.
Don't stop eating. Don't stop eating. Don't stop eating.

Don't stop eating. Don't stop eating. Don't stop eating.
Don't stop eating. Don't stop eating. Don't stop eating.
Don't stop eating. Don't stop eating. Don't stop eating.
Don't stop eating. Don't stop eating. Don't stop eating.
Don't stop eating. Don't stop eating. Don't stop eating.
Don't stop eating. Don't stop eating. Don't stop eating.
Don't stop eating. Don't stop eating. Don't stop eating.
Don't stop eating. Don't stop eating. Don't stop eating.
Don't stop eating. Don't stop eating. Don't stop eating.
Don't stop eating. Don't stop eating. Don't stop eating.
Don't stop eating. Don't stop eating. Don't stop eating.
Don't stop eating. Don't stop eating. Don't stop eating.
Don't stop eating. Don't stop eating. Don't stop eating.
Don't stop eating. Don't stop eating. Don't stop eating.
Don't stop eating. Don't stop eating. Don't stop eating.
Don't stop eating. Don't stop eating. Don't stop eating.
Don't stop eating. Don't stop eating. Don't stop eating.
Don't stop eating. Don't stop eating. Don't stop eating.
Don't stop eating. Don't stop eating. Don't stop eating.
Don't stop eating. Don't stop eating. Don't stop eating.
Don't stop eating. Don't stop eating. Don't stop eating.
Don't stop eating. Don't stop eating. Don't stop eating.
Don't stop eating. Don't stop eating. Don't stop eating.
Don't stop eating. Don't stop eating. Don't stop eating.
Don't stop eating. Don't stop eating. Don't stop eating.
Don't stop eating. Don't stop eating. Don't stop eating.
Don't stop eating. Don't stop eating. Don't stop eating.
Don't stop eating. Don't stop eating. Don't stop eating.
Don't stop eating. Don't stop eating. Don't stop eating.
Don't stop eating. Don't stop eating. Don't stop eating.
Don't stop eating. Don't stop eating. Don't stop eating.
Don't stop eating. Don't stop eating. Don't stop eating.
Don't stop eating. Don't stop eating. Don't stop eating.
Don't stop eating. Don't stop eating. Don't stop eating.
Don't stop eating. Don't stop eating. Don't stop eating.

Pretending. Sometimes that's all it takes to be good at life, huh?

I was always shit at that.

Don't know how long it's been since I've eaten, but it's starting to get warm outside again. I've survived on peanut butter smoothies. Everything else is a miss. I try stuffing my face with hot dogs or burgers to get something more solid in me, and end up throwing up a vile mass, iridescent and seafoam green. The inside of an alien, not a woman.

In place of sleep and appetite, dark thoughts take over my days.

Tonight, I am taking the shape of a wild animal, out on a midnight stroll. The cracked pavement leads me to thinking about danger, about bad decisions. They're the only good ones I seem to make. What if? What if I was really here? How do I prove I exist? I think about dropping a pack of gum or an ear of corn on the street. I imagine a small dog, a Bichon Frisé or a great dane, finding it on their miserable, urban walks. What if the owner, unaware, lets an hour pass? Ignores the signs? What if the dog dies? All that power is in my hands if I wanted. I could simply leave the scene. I could exist. I could be an existence with consequence.

After all, bad things of consequence exist all around us. Cloud has shown me this truth. Bad foods, rotten foods, foods we are fools to ingest. In my sleeplessness, I have become wise to the poison around us. The city is full of it. Iris—I can't let Iris become a place of impurity. Bad ingredients, processed junk. Maybe in all my madness, I have become a zealot. I have become a messenger. Antonia the Saint!

More walking until my feet hurt, then I stop at a 24-hour diner. It's better than being home. Home's where the temptation of skin picking or worse could tear into me at any moment. I prefer my sins hidden behind beautiful exteriors. Like this overpriced diner. A bell chimes when I stroll in—don't mind me. I'm a puffy blur disguised as a woman. A creature with no place to go. Plus, the clubs are closed now, it'll be a few more hours before the first senior citizen comes in for the early-bird special. I won't take up much space.

Besides, I like the vibes of this joint. They don't seem to mind if I stay here for hours, reading cookbooks or brainstorming recipe ideas. Oh, to taste freshly peeled garlic again! Weird how I get more creative with hunger. Saint Antonia, the hungry chef!

I take up my preferred spot in the corner of the room, near the bathrooms. I like it here. The old man usually leaves a mop dripping into a once-yellow bucket after he washes up. But there's someone new here today: a balding man with a thick accent, yelling at the lonely line cook in the back. He shoots me a stare like he knows all. Knows I'm up to no good. No matter. By now, I've developed a system.

Order toast, anything that travels well and won't look too hideous. Minimal decay. I let the plate cool in front of me. Let the eggs develop a glaze. The only thing I can't get over is the smell. Every time I have gone out to buy a vaporub pen, the stores are closed, so I have opted for dabbing some of my carry-on toothpaste under my nose before I eat. Ghastly business—that I have to practice breathing and chewing at the same time, like some inhuman oddity.

In front of me is a pamphlet I swiped from the counter for an organic farm, just upstate. One of those ads that's been collecting dust for years. I flip through its contents and make out the name Drake Farms. There's a drawing of a green field, happy cows. I wonder if that's true. Are cows happy anywhere in the human consumption business? Something to look at later, for my recipes. How does joy taste?

Eventually, I can't keep up the pretense any longer. I pay for the food, leave it there, and leave.

I regret not buying a corn on the cob.

It was night and then it isn't.

When I open my eyes, the room spins. Only the ceiling is not the popcorned mess in my room, it's the domed arches back at Iris. My face is wet. I look down and smell the awful stench of a distorted, alien red onion, and quickly realize the tears are my own.

I need Cloud. I *long* for Cloud. Just a wisp. Something to take the edge off. To sleep the time away.

The crew doesn't notice my quiet freakout, since they're all diligently preparing for dinner.

The splendor of Iris is made small by the foul smells. But in my logical senses, I know it is pristine. Vanilla-white domes, punctured by industrial lights. Dark lines of metal raised above each station. Three on either side. Airy and light, just the way Mika and I planned. The imported ovens, decked in copper, with a line of pans hung overhead. My shoes squeak on the waxed floor—a floor I've hand scrubbed so many times before. Clean enough to eat off of. Lionel is fixing something at the front of the restaurant, and I can see his calm smile through the slate gap facing the dining room. "If Restoration Hardware had a soul," Mika once joked. He'll be moving onto watering the plants next, something we argued about for weeks before I gave in. Oddly enough, it's the only thing in here that doesn't stink. Purity, I think.

"Rody, what time is it?"

I catch myself.

"I mean, *Amir*, what time is it?

"Lost track of time, Chef?"

"Something like that . . . "

"You've been here since I got here, boss, so 10 am or so?"

My eyes narrow in on the assortment of pots behind him, blurring the rest. I make a mental note to reapply toothpaste under my nose.

"Hmm," I reply, and he goes back to his work.

I've been here all night. Already my pants feel wet with damp sweat and reminds me I haven't done laundry in some time. I can smell the diner toast under my fingertips.

Massie knows something's up, as girls that age intrinsically know things but are seldom given credit for. She throws me a troubled look, then shoots one at Eddie. Lionel comes in from the wash-up room, unsure of what to say. He flees to the office, where Mika sits on the chair, talking distractedly on the phone. Thursday. Vegetable supplier, I think.

He cups the receiver and hears Lionel out. Now they both look at me. I pretend not to notice and take note instead of the clientele coming in, wide-eyed and well-dressed, trying not to be amazed at the splendor of oak lined walls and custard-colored seating. We're not at the tourist drop yet.

On the wall, there are menu updates scribbled in Mika's cursive—the bottles we're pushing and desserts du jour. One of the hostesses has drawn smilies on the plates' descriptions.

I zoom around to the stations, pacing back and forth to get a sense of the quality. Part of me can sense there's some tension, but it doesn't feel like agitation. A vacuum of control, the negation of the body before an anticipated fall, the catch in your voice before it breaks. The quivering unbending of a lover before they sever the relationship. I shoot Mika a look. I remember, I forget. My body longs for a space—real or simulated. A place I can touch something, eat something, and have it return the favor. Antonia the Saint has no followers. I study Mike again in his resolution. He's gathering information from dishes, what should be changed, what to replace. Spices that feel off tonight. Tables needing more care. An anniversary party we should send a special dessert out to. The whole ritual throws me off kilter. I am looking at my life passing me by, and I cannot get in. Whether this was the state of things before Cloud is immaterial. The feeling props my body up like a flesh-tent, hollowed out to make space for the prenominal sadness. Act out reality, Antonia. My focus returns, at great cost to my limbs, leadenly pulling at the joints. I inspect dishes left and right. I pretend.

Mika makes his way over to me. Both of us crowd Amir, who's hunched over like a crab.

"Hey Antonia, didn't know you were staying."

"Why wouldn't I?"

There's a brief silence, and I can hear the record player skipping around. Mika lets me feel the silence as an admonishment for my behavior. As if this isn't my restaurant.

"No, no, of course. It's actually good you came in. Follow me."

With that, I follow him to my office and the kitchen resumes its usual banter. Massie goes up to the record player, adjusting the disc.

Inside my office, it smells like men. I make a point to yank open the drawer and reach for one of my candles. This is not your space. I light the match, and stand between him and the chairs.

Once the candle is lit, we sit on the two armchairs, away from my desk. It's the proper thing to do when you're filling in for someone and you're about to tell them off.

"What do you think you're doing?"

"Uh, it's my place. I can—"

"I know it's your place. Our place. But we agreed I'd take over for now. You signed the papers."

"What?"

"It's nothing formal. It's for your security. You're taking time off."

We sit in silence, but it's not clicking. The days are a sealed-off tomb of memories.

"I'm making sure no one is slacking," I say through gritted teeth.

"Well, don't. Don't worry. We're fine. No one is tarnishing Iris's reputation or yours. And slacking? Have you met these guys?"

He gestures with his eyes to the staff, feigning a smile and other gestures for the appearance of things.

"Hmm."

I try to push this paranoia out of my head but I can't recall signing any papers. I can't trust myself either. The food outside is starting to smell. One hand on my arm now, he leans in to ask me something. I can tell he's eaten and it's repulsive. There's decay on his breath, the bacteria of meat taking up residence in his mouth. I pull away. I don't want to be contaminated. No candle is strong enough to rid myself of the stench.

"You really okay?

"Yeah." I just need to get away from his smell.

"You're no good to us in pieces."

"Fine."

He rubs his legs, uncomfortably.

"Can I get one of those clips?"

I point to the paper clips on his calendar desk.

"Uh, sure."

He hands me one and I pocket it.

Outside in the alley, I clip my loose jeans. No need to make much of it. They were loose to begin with. A balmy spring evening condenses into my pores. More to pick at later. The weather would be nice except for the putrid smells coming up from the restaurant corridor, enticing the filthy hungers in our bodies.

A shape appears in the alley.

"Toni."

*Ugh.*

The figure solidifies into the elf. Mister Booth. His boyish grin looks jackal-mad in the pale blue light.

"You left this at Fames." He hands me my wallet, reading the expression on my face. "Oh, you don't remember. "

"I forget a lot lately. Don't take it personally."

"You came in last night."

"I thought you were in Spain."

"Toni, we already had this conversation."

"Of course," I say, scanning the ground while I rummage through the wall of memory loss. There's a slight stench in the air and I can't seem to shake it. If I get my hands on more Cloud, some of it is bound to come back. Or . . . I can time travel. I can skip over years of my life. I don't have to be present when I disappear.

"Are you joining us today?"

"I want to, but I don't think I have the energy." My teeth chatter.

"Sure. I understand. You've had a long day. See you around."

And then he disappears.

I fidget with the clip and pocket my wallet, but there's something there.

A bag full of Cloud.

In another lifetime, Alice and I leave the club early. We go to a late-night coffee shop and discuss books, our slow-bloomer lifestyles. The night goes well and we go home and shower. She reads me her favorite quotes from Jeanette Winterson. We make love. I don't lose myself in the relationship. We both get stronger, together, maybe rent a little flat in the city and adopt a cat. We go to Mika and Hannah's wedding. I move on.

In another lifetime, our worlds unite, not fracture.

# ACT III

**T**HE TRIP TO Aunt Jo's house across the state is not planned. I get up in the middle of the night, my sleep all fucked up from taking Cloud in the afternoon, and I pack a bag. Mostly, I am in need of centering myself. Reminding myself that I exist at all.

*This is a gift*, I keep thinking. If I were someone else, I'd know how to use it correctly. There are lines in my head about pure food and our rotten hunger but I don't have the strength to put it together. A chef prodigy is only as good as their output.

The plan is simple: visit the farm in the brochure, then stop at my Aunt Jo's house. I pull out the pamphlet from the diner. It still smells like bad hamburger meat. The green font curls up on a frame of a red farmhouse and neverending green fields: Drake Farms—forty minutes north of the city.

According to the brochure, the farm has been in the Drakes' hands for generations, managing to escape the wave of farmer suicides and corporate snakes which plagued farmlands across the nation in the late 90s. The key to their success was hard to emulate, according to the marketer. Mainly, they'd hitched their success to the sleepy hollow of Liney, bringing a humble, cosmopolitan center to what had once been rural oil territory.

The restaurants, butcher, small artisan shops, farmers' markets, all rely on Drake Farms, and so they secured a livelihood there. The eldest Drake son married a wealthy woman from Montana, per my googling, supposedly skilled in business and all that junk. Organic, pesticide-free, free-range. Drake Farms had escaped the great machine, and they were my last hope.

By now, my hallucinations are almost 24/7. I can feel the truth of everything taking over. I am fading out of this world and into Saint Antonia's. The decay has spread from food to roads, cars, marks left by humans who have touched food. The world lights up like one of those true crime blue light scenes. Cloud's filter has become the only one, no toggle off button. Life is now gray and metallic, in a desperate search for color. For light.

There's a fastidiousness to my rituals, a jitteriness. I stomp in and out of rooms, half-aware of what I am doing.

This morning, for instance, I find my body time-traveled to the bathroom. I'm mid-brushing my hair with one of those expensive brushes, a birthday gift from Mika. A ballet pink handle with thick boar bristles shooting off the matte-white center. The bespoke logo in cursive at the bottom. My hair is flatter these days, and the upside to that is it is more manageable. I stroke through the back. The brush is heavier than I remember, but I've also lost more weight. The number on the scale is in the double-digits. My head feels like taffy, and when I brush through the ends, there's a large clump of red hair in my hands. I let out a whimper, and touch the thinning scalp. How unfair is it to lose the hair that matters and look down at the fur growing on my arms? I pin my hair down and look in the mirror. It's gone from auburn to brown. I don't have the energy to cry, so I simply turn off the lights.

Still, my mood today is better than most days. I sit in a chair and put on my shoes, which takes great effort. Every limb is leaden. Left foot done. Right foot done. I curse myself for not buying slip-on shoes. I'm whatever is beyond exhausted.

The only clothes I feel remotely human in are Mika's old sweater and a pair of black leggings. Everything falls down to my ankles. The worst thing is when my underwear kept falling. Talk about annoying. I've gone commando for a few months now. There's nothing to worry about since I don't recall the last period I had. I grab a bag, my favorite knife, and a grocery bag along with some cash. As I said, I have high hopes. A notification blinks on my phone. The first line: *Status of Iris; from Mika.* I swipe the notification off and go downstairs.

# A FEAST OF PUTRID DELIGHTS

Outside, the air feels bleak. It's rained the night before, and the night before that, and the earth smells of it. I avoid looking at the heaps of decay and glittering, alien-like gunk along the sideway. The impurity. I take a taxi to Mika's apartment, on the other edge of the city. I'm too tired to exert myself by running to catch the subway. Besides, there's more filth to worry about there. While I wait for the car to arrive, I huddle my scarf around my head, taking in the blue sunrise.

When the cab approaches, Mika's already outside, next to his car. My mind goes to Hannah, upstairs in their apartment, telling him not to let me up. I can barely remember what their apartment looks like. Last time I was here, he was having a New Year's Eve party for the staff. Everyone commented on how clean it all was. Usually, chefs spend so much time at our places that homes become an after-thought. Mika beamed as she told us about Hannah's impeccable taste. A few of us even took pictures.

The driver opens my door without a sound. Part of me feels guilty for not speaking, but also his gray aura is so strong, I have to focus to keep from throwing up. The man is covered in decay. Many hands have touched him. Children, maybe. A loving wife. Hands that touch hands, that touch food, that are living beings. How can I reconcile the truth of the world—decay—with how we live? Is this man racing towards rot with the spoiled world he touches daily? There's a sourness to the city, a new-found danger in the poison everywhere. I cannot avoid it. I want to warn everyone. I do not have the words. The truth is there. How do I warn everyone that they're prey for decay?

Mika waves but does not hug me, further confirmation that Hannah is in one of the windows, spying on us. He jingles a set of keys and plops them into my hands.

"Thanks, I'll probably have it back by tomorrow."

He shrugs me off, like a guy.

"Don't sweat it. We're staying in all weekend to paint the nursery."

"Oh, that's nice," I say, unconvincingly.

Before I can come up with something sweeter, Mika turns up the street, waving me off without looking.

"Have fun!"

Mika, like the rest of the staff, assumes I'm headed to a camp for nutrition and wellness. By this point, they are sure I have developed an eating disorder. I'm fine with this. It's easier to explain than seeing a new dimension, the matrix, or whatever it is Cloud opened my eyes to.

The ziploc bag floats in my pocket.

The ride up to the farm is pretty boring, though cleaner than the city. There's less poison here, less decay, but more often than not, it's a different sort of decay—sluggish, heavy. I recognize the failure of duality in truth here. The highway is decayed with green moss and a russet-colored, fleshy, pulsing wall of dead mammals. A long stretch of highway, the spring sun wetting the sky with light, collides with this reality. In spite of this, I feel focused and ready.

Drake Farms is a white trimmed, green stretch of land off the highway. The vast open space feels more like Louisiana or Arkansas than upstate. Trees nestle my car down the road, until I hit a lone metal gate and a sign that reads, "ORGANIC".

Before I can make it out, a woman signals me through gates up ahead. She's prettier than I thought a "farmer" would look, like a young Cherry Jones, with brown hair that hits just above her shoulders. I turn the car in, hearing the wiper match the pace of the rain patter. The woman doesn't seem to mind the weather and I like her immediately for this. I park in front of the field, a huge expanse of land. On the horizon, a brown building dots the liquid blue sky. *Look up, Antonia, look up and you won't notice the decay.*

The woman's name is Diane, quite a coincidence, and her dogs are Pippin and Frodo.

"My husband loves all that Tolkien stuff," she says, throwing her head back to me. I'm lagging a few steps behind. "It's really great having a chef from the city up here. How did you hear about us? It's just a short walk this way."

"I'm glad you took the call from an urban dweller."

"Of course. Sounds like destiny, doesn't it?"

I answer a few questions, worn out by her energy. I lie and claim a waiter from a nearby restaurant told me where the food was sourced. This appears to please her. Better than telling her I found her info at the back of a diner.

We take a tour of the crop fields, past a field of sunflowers. At least, I have to take her word for it. To me, they're fighting specks of unborn amphibians, falling from the sky. A Boschian hellscape narrowing in on this oasis.

"We do a maze for the kids in the fall," she explains.

Damp earth and soured mulch hit my nose as we turn into the farm's line of sight. Cows gather below, flicking flies while a large orange tractor stops behind them. I don't know if it's Diane or the adrenaline being so close to a stretch of pure earth, but everything starts filling with color. Less alien junk.

In the middle of our conversation, I've become another person.

"Oh this is great. Smell that!" I let out. It's the first real smell I can appreciate in a while.

"Yeah?" Diane chuckles. "Takes a wise person to appreciate good manure."

Excitedly, I lean in to examine a pile of fresh dung. No radioactive film or iridescent goo. Then we turn our attention to the cows.

"You're happy gals, huh?" I glance over at Diane who nods and we both touch the cow's face, feeling its coarse hair bristle against our skin.

Diane looks pleased, and all of a sudden, all I want to do is please Diane. I want this to work, to cure me, to set Iris apart from the gunky food-poison everywhere.

"So this is the same stuff used to fertilize your crops?"

"Yes ma'am. We like to keep it all-natural here. And

folks will tell you, it shows in our crops. These are happy cows. They have happy shits. And we get happy crops. No pesticides. This is why, if you'll see, we bought out the next two fields. Over 15 acres. The shitty thing about chemicals is, even if you don't use them, your neighbor pollutes your own farm along with theirs." She shakes her head.

"It's pure poison."

"Damn straight."

She gets closer to me and we pet the cow again, whose name I learn is Lulu. I tuck myself out of Diane's reach, careful not to be too close to smell what she'd eaten last. I didn't take her for someone who ate just anything, but I had to be certain.

By the time we hit the fields, my legs wobble under me like atrophied potatoes. The car is barely a dot in the landscape, though the sun reflects like a night star off its roof. Diane has suggested a light lunch before I leave, which I half-agreed to, but by the end of the farm tour, I can tell she's wary of me, arms outstretched whenever I move—as if she can see whatever ails me is taking over.

The cows and horses are divided by another barn, a smaller coop than the others.

"Chickens," Diane informs me.

The crops are limited since they'd just started planting for spring. Wheat and corn are the mainstays. I kneel to touch the fresh soil, aware of a new buzzing sound in my ears. The music of Fames, I think. The first night I met Booth, everyone was dancing in an otherworldly stupor. Low notes and hums from the earth.

I look down at the rough elements between my fingers. Small bits of dung and dirt and nutrients, tiny stones of growth. It's speaking to me. I shake my head.

"Nice, yes, very nice."

Then—

"You know, I've been sick. Some autoimmune thing. I can't help but think it's something in the food."

"Yes, it's all the food! I'm so sorry to hear it . . . " Her reply sounds like she already knew, and this confirms it.

"This is why we understand each other, Diane. This is personal." I surprise myself. I'd never talked like that before in my life. Mika, Mika spoke like that.

By the end of the road, we've seen most of it. Now we're standing in the shadows of Diane's southern house, white and gray, more greenhouse than human living space. The dogs are resting on the patio, looking up at us. In lieu of lunch, Diane has prepared a crate of fresh vegetables and eggs to take back with me. "Think of it as a sample case," she tells me. We look out at the great expanse of farmland. The bosh elements have faded into the gathering dark.

"Well?"

"Thank you for giving me the tour, I think . . . We'd love to work together."

"The start of a relationship. Thrilled to hear it."

"Now, I'm going to need to bring my partner by before we sign anything. Would that be okay?"

"Bring as many as you want!" And then, "I can have one of my sons take the golf cart and bring you back to your car."

In a moment of pure madness, I turn from the view and smile back at her. "You know, if it's okay with you, I'd love to walk back. Such a pretty walk."

Diane considers me momentarily, but given my general pallor, she concludes I'm not a threat.

"Alright. Take care." And she watches me leave.

Before long, I'm in the middle of the field, the red coop in my sights. My body is hitting 1%. It's been a couple of hours since my last meal and the mood swings are coming on full force. The sounds of field bugs irritate me. The patch of sweat forming on the small of my back feels unbearably wet and icky, leaving me with the desire to rip my whole sweater off and strip naked. The feeling gnaws. Still, I manage to get caught up in the music of the countryside. Crickets, small birds, chickens.

When I pass the chicken coop, something catches my attention. A lone pig, munching on hay. My body is overtaken by an animalistic urge. I'm hungry. So hungry.

The pig eyes me, or I think it does. A small snort and it rounds away from me, towards the chickens. But, no matter. She's backed herself into a corner now. Dumb thing.

There's no way out. My boots sink into the damp soil, scattered with yellow-brown pellets. The whole space smells of shit and animals. Fucking wonderful. My eyes dry and I realize I've forgotten to blink. Hands spread out in front of me, I touch the barn air as if I expect resistance. Dews of sweat drip off my nose. Salty. Primal. The chase draws near. I have become the feral thing. I enter the barn through a broken part of the wall, stepping into a puddle of bluish, iridescent hay.

When I look up, the ceiling is Jupiter blue—a galaxy of stars, ocean creatures with glittering tentacles, open mouths, and kaleidoscopes. *God is with me,* I think, but the thought could not have come from me. Me, raised in a proudly questioning house with my auntie. Me, doing whatever I want with my temple. Me, so very hungry. I wipe the sweat off my lip before it can slide any farther down my neck, and corner the creature.

She's panicked now, moving left and right in the small prison she's made for herself. In her stare, I find only fear. Whatever animal communication she attempts remains unopened to me. Not that I care any longer. This is my chance. Thinking I hear a twig break, or footsteps, I jerk my neck towards the door, half-expecting Diane Drake or one of her broad-shouldered boys to ruin this for me.

You must understand. By this point, it's been three months since I had pork, or meat of any kind. Weeks since I've had more than a cup of anything solid. And here is this pig, a soft gentle thing. A gift from the gods. *No, a test.*

Taking care to not make any sudden movements, I unzip my purse by leaning it against my side. The case of the blade pelts against my rib cage. When I unsheathe it, centering it between my knuckles, the pig starts to whine. She patterns in a circle again, an intelligent thing, feeling this is her end.

A few feet from us, chickens balk. I can no longer see them. Only her. The pig finally faces me. She's gray, but a beautiful natural gray, with white hairs dotting her snout and chin, and darker spots on her backside. Two velvet ears listening for me, acting like a second pair of eyes. Her torso is medium-sized, probably a young adult. I wonder for a split-second where the others might be hiding. I wonder if they've sensed this one is in danger, like those moms on those true crime documentaries who swear they feel when their kids draw their last breaths.

Everything is connected. We are all simply too caught up in our own violent little stories to make any sense of it. I inch up closer, buckling my knees on either side of her until she's practically mounted. My boots slide and she squirms under my grip. When I grab her ears, she squeals up at me, her large eyes expressive and fearful.

Above me, the ceiling whispers, urging me on. I raise my knife from my boots above my head ceremonially to show my strength, and slide it into the perfect grip. But she skitters away, shrieking.

"Quiet, you!"

I'm on the floor, speckled with blue mud.

My knees ache as I rise. Squatting, I corral her into another part of the barn. The chase commences again. Her mouth opens wide, saliva pouring out from both sides. A creature in terror. A creature, a gift for her god. I jab forward. The knife tears at her large snout. Her cries are deafening now. I need to act fast. The red of her blood is the only vibrant color in the room. *More, gimme more.* She slips again so I kick her in the stomach. Finally, she's under me—a god on a horse. I strike the knife down at her back surgically, touching around at the fat on either side of her spine. All I need is a bit of help.

I cut a square formation, nothing too deep, which elicits a horrible cry from the pig. Will Diane hear us? I don't mind anymore. I kick the pig again because I need her alive. I drop to my knees, buckling her again so she'll stop squirming. The knife slips.

*Fuck it all.* I bite down where I made the cut.

Delicious. Ecstasy. Unbelievably fresh and pure. My mouth is full of blood and the warm juice of her body. Forbidden fruit, like a giant gummy bear with everlasting flavor inside.

The pig squeals again, though I'm too far gone to hear it. New blood drools out the corners of my mouth and I am free. I emerge from the barn a different color, the purifying red of gore.

A day later, I find myself at my aunt's house. The front is unchanged and there are new roses in the pots near the door. I peel back the welcome mat, but she's moved the key.

Strange.

No matter. I'll go in through the back door. Nasty piece of work. The thing was always creaking open in the middle of the night. Used to scare us both to death. Sure enough, the mauve screen door in the back opens and behind it, the door is unlocked. There's a terrible smell coming from the kitchen, so I sniff my way upstairs to safety. But it's rather a confusing state inside. It's all changed—inside organs aged and the outside covered up with fine paint. She'd redecorated before her death? Possibly, though Aunt Jo never liked change. The floral couch is gone. In its place is a lifeless leather couch, pale blue, layered with chemise blankets. It all feels like a Model Home exhibit, lifeless and tacky.

My room is changed, as well. It looks like an office. Aunt Jo never was one for computers, which is unnerving because there are two towers near the window. I look around for our boxes but don't find any, only hiking gear and old sweaters.

In the corner is a file cabinet next to a mirror. One peek inside tells me there's nothing there for me. I catch myself standing in front of the mirror, aghast. My weight is unfamiliar to me, a new heaviness filling my hollow flesh. My skin is blotchy. I don't recognize myself. I stick out my tongue, the only part of me with good color nowadays. *Thank you, o' Drake Farms pig.* I'll have to think of how to get down there on the way back. There's a clarity to me I can't describe. Something beyond this world.

In the hallway, I pull the attic string in the hallway and plunge the ladder down to the carpet. Each step up takes a great deal of effort. This part of the house looks untouched, just how I remember it. Aunt Jo's flashlights hang off the door, and I sling one around my neck.

In the corner of the attic, a large box labeled *"journals, cookbooks, and photo albums"* in my aunt's handwriting sits in the corner. I blow off the dust and open the lid. I'm perplexed because the first thing I see is pamphlets with rainbows on them.

*"Understanding Bisexuality."*

*"Love is Acceptance; you and your child."*

I let out a cry and sit there, fingers trembling over the paper.

The morning after the bombing at Pixel my aunt Jo called me "on a hunch". She knew my luck—my history of being in places I shouldn't be. She was not a dense woman, even though her glamorous old-lady fashion and manner of talking made people underestimate her.

"You and I are more alike than you think, missy," she used to tell me on days when I felt extra sour towards authority. What did they know, anyway, my teachers and classmates? Life was so easy for them—drowning in the suburban daze of after-school sports, fro-yo runs, Sunday church.

Meanwhile, my aunt and I would drive back into the city in her teal convertible with the top down, to camp out at some weird friend's house lined with naked art and photographs of places far away.

In those days, I had a history of being at the wrong place at the wrong time, like I said. On scene at a drug deal near the playground, hiding in the basement during a carbon monoxide leak, along with the neighbor's cat. You name it. My early childhood was a minefield of dangerous encounters, and with each incident, my aunt added a few more gray hairs to her collection. Once, she was sitting on the couch with me, pulling at some strands, and said, "Look, the Antonia collection."

On the morning of the shooting, I wasn't particularly up for talking to anyone, but I never screened my aunt's calls. When my cell rang, I was laid out on the bed, looking at the ceiling.

"Antonia? Thank Jesus. Have you seen the news? Oh, this is just awful. Oh!"

Our conversations always started halfway through a topic. It was as if she was poking her head into my bedroom, glass full of brown liquid, rollers in her hair, manicured nails playing with one of her strange amulet necklaces.

"Let me look. What channel?" I flicked the crust out of my eyes and put her on speaker.

"4. Oh my god. These poor kids," Aunt Jo lamented.

I pulled up the local site on my phone and played the video, as if it was news to me. There it was—the warehouse. I could smell it just by looking at the screen. The newscaster kept speaking as the b-roll panned over to the entrance; the words PIXEL, dinged with smoke. The headline read:

**"ATTACK ON PIXEL: LGBTQA+ HATE CRIME"**

"Did you know anyone?" she asked. I could hear her dragging on her morning cigarette.

"No. No, I didn't," I lied.

"Oh my god. Just awful."

There was a pause between us.

"Well, just wanted to see if you're okay. Awful stuff down there."

I tried to tell her this sort of stuff happened everywhere now. Aunt Jo muttered a few choice adjectives about our governor and asked me for the hundredth time if I didn't want to move back upstate with her. This time, I considered it. I didn't have much keeping me here. Just a string of service jobs, a cheap rent that was no longer cheap, and Mika. The thought of him appearing upstate made me feel like a teenager again.

"I'm okay."

She'd known. I'm overtaken by a new wave of guilt. How lonely she must have been. How selfish I had been while she was alive.

I fold the pamphlets and stick them in my pockets, and flip through the folders.

Then I see it.

The newspaper from that day.

My greasy fingers smudge the headlines. I open it up and see a face I've seen before. A white-haired young man with a lopsided grin and dead eyes. Under the photo is the caption: *Bomber*, but it looks like *Booth* I shake the paper to break the illusion, but which is which?

"Who's there?" an alarmed voice echoes up to the attic and it is assuredly not my aunt's.

Is someone else living here now? My mind is fuzzy with details—a realtor, a neglected call.

In spite of my current state, I jump down the ladder and make eye contact with a very puzzled looking man. He's not shouting, only clutching what looks like a notepad. He seems to know my face, though I do not know his. The person next to him screams and I make a run for it. The man's feet thunder my way, but with that stench, I'll be able to know when he's out of sight.

Something buzzes by the sink. I ignore the message, letting it go to voicemail. The phone buzzes again, then falls dark.

Outside my apartment, a bleak chill pushes way up my

ankles and against my legs. I disappear in my puffer coat, looking something like a malnourished beetle.

My stomach pangs with an insatiable hunger. The soles of my feet slap against the pavement. Everything hurts. I should have taken that pig. I should have killed Diane and eaten all those chickens. I bump into an older woman and excuse myself. She grunts, and I move aside. I turn back in the direction I was walking, towards a park I used to visit where old women practice yoga. He's nearby, I think. There's no contemplation in my revelation. Only clarity.

I stagger in the vertigo of the city buildings, their spires touching the soft blue sky. The wonder of their many histories is a worthy antidote to my newfound paranoia. A parade of school-age children passes me, tied together with a pink leash, led by a soft-looking young woman. She coos to them as they cross the street, gossiping among one another. Kids in the city never fail to amaze me. They look out of place, like flowers in an abandoned lot. Hopeful living things, wandering a space unkind to humans.

The park entrance is already bursting with food vendors, prepping for the early lunch crowd of nannies and college kids. The street carts selling gyros and hot dogs catch my attention first, because of the odor. To my surprise, the worst offender comes from the sweet roasted nuts, which reeks of an unclean belly button.

I rush past them, then walk aimlessly through the park until stumbling upon a smoothie cart. After scanning the menu, my nose buried in my jacket, I settle on the Peanut Butter Dream smoothie. Calories are the name of the game now.

A few blocks later, Booth's comes into view. The plan is starting to take shape. I am so close to finding out the truth. And Cloud can only help. I cross the street and duck into the lobby behind a tenant, revitalized by the protein in my smoothie. Under the doorbell, I narrow in on his name.

There it is—**B Hendricks.**

I push the beige button, retreating my hand and squeezing through my black gloves. The thing crackles, static forming into a voice.

"Yes?" Booth sounds less chipper than last time we spoke.

"Hey, it's me. Antonia. Let me up."

"Toni! still mad at me?"

"I'm not here to bust your balls. I know it isn't your fault."

"The road to hell is paved with . . . well, come on up—"

A pause.

"But let's keep our pants on."

The electric metal gate unlatches with a loud buzz.

The door opens to reveal Booth, half-dressed in a dark indigo kimono, loose gray joggers, no shirt. He's in a theatrical mood. Loves playing characters, this one. His face snags into an Edward Norton grin. He has less hair on his chest than he thinks he does and the confidence of someone who has probably seen too many 80s films. I repress the cruel observations and manage a smile, meeting his gaze.

"You look terrible," he says.

His mouth forms a frown of disgust, curling into his long upper lip. I give him a sarcastic *thank you* and tell him I've been better. Although, I can no longer remember what that feels like.

Pre-Cloud, pre-insomnia, pre-Pixel, pre-Iris. The self-deprecation seems to convince him of something and he leads me inside, closing the door behind us. I can't help but keep looking at him. Trying to remember what happened that night at Pixel. Can it be?

He casts a dark glance at me and waves his long bony hands around, watching me intently. I'm no good at small talk, so I scan the room for something to chat about. Over at the fridge, I pick at the magnets, playing with a Shiba Inu rocket magnet. Someone else, maybe Booth, has glued on googly eyes.

"So what do you want, Antonia? Last time I heard from you, all I got was screaming and bitching."

I throw him a stare.

"I'd rather sleep than eat. That's really it. I need more."

"You know, Delilah thinks the stuff activated you or something. Made you unstable."

The painter, I think.

Booth is closer to me now, his tone almost flirtatious. I cannot bear to think that I look like his type, or anyone else's. I remember the newspaper image and shudder. He leans in, too close for comfort, and points at a snowman magnet.

"That one there is my favorite."

A chill prickles along my neck. "I can't imagine why Delilah would think so. We got on so well," I say coyly, surprising myself. I pull out a wad of cash. "Will this do—?"

The art of not saying things is kind of my calling, I think. Booth gives me another whiff, like a dog, and zones in on the cash. His expression shifts from excitement to contemplation. The gears are turning. He's wondering if he can convince me to give him my body as well as my money. Booth takes the money gently and sinks his hands into his robe.

"Of course. I'm a gentleman."

He gives me a wink, retreating towards a smaller wall, framed by a red chest. There's a hate burning inside me and nowhere for it to go.

"And for you, I'll get the fresh stuff."

When he leans down to the last drawer, I see his aura radiate around him. The vision of Booth, surrounded by a ghostly gray coloring, captivates me. I don't continue the small talk, or make an effort to appear normal.

His aura is lovely, I admit to myself. Peaceful, with a glimmer of Cloud moving inside his bloodstream. There's a shimmer when it flows to the center of his heart, milky white with specks of turquoise. He hasn't eaten this morning. I can smell it. I consider whether I can really get away with this next part. I have to. For everyone at Pixel.

# A FEAST OF PUTRID DELIGHTS

As Booth fumbles, I inch nearer. The red chest is carved with vines, and adorned with gold bats. It looks custom made, expensive. A mulberry piece of fabric, velvety and silk, bulges out of the last drawer. In between the cushions, there it is—a whole drawer full of Cloud. Booth rises to his feet, holding a fresh Ziploc bag. It seems strange seeing an item of purity in a baggie made for Oreos or loose paper clips. The wispy dandelions float in the bag, as if they were fully dense, and take up space. My mouth waters. Booth notices this and throws me a knowing smile.

"I gave you three grand," I croak.

Booth's eyes sink, suddenly seriously.

"And you'll get your money's worth. As soon as you're done, you can come on by for the next batch. Think of this as a retainer. And my holding back as a mark of our friendship. Besides, I like your company. We've missed you at Fames."

My eyes dart to the drawer. I don't need anyone in my way now, especially the one who caused this mess in the first place. I let the quiet make him uncomfortable. The room feels suffocatingly small. In an effort to appease me, Booth extends his hand, relinquishing the drugs. He smiles softly and heads across the room to the bar, picking up a gold tumbler. The coffee table next to the couch is swimming in odd pastries, all of which have a tint of decay to them—feather at the edges and moldy inside. The only distinct object I can make out is a large snail fossil, almost the size of my head.

"You're something special, Antonia . . . What have you been doing with your gift?" He smiles derisively.

Booth draws another glass, rimmed with gold, and pours the concoction from the tumbler. I'm mindful of my steps, which barely creak as I pace towards him. Over his shoulder, I hover. He's curling an orange peel with one of those boutique specialty knives, expensive without cause. At the sight of the fruit, I'm overcome with a sudden rage as it shifts into a milky white fungus, How can he not know he's eating poison? A dark cloud of madness floods my head. My veins pulse on the right side of my neck, heated in anticipation. In a split-second, I've become too powerful.

"Drink with me," he says, turning around with drinks in hand.

"Sure thing." I seethe.

But I do not smile. I do not take the cup. Instead, I lift the giant fossil from his coffee table and smash his face. The sound of his sharp exhale echoes in my mind. He collapses, forehead bouncing off the edge of the bar.

Spatters of blood speckle the teal rug, sinking into its soft tentacles. His body doesn't move. It just lies there, flopped up and heavy. The broken glasses lay at my feet. I recover my breath, set the bloody fossil down, and bend over him. I extend a finger, poke his face from the rug towards me. A large gash on his forehead bleeds profusely, saturating his hair at the temple. He's dead. Or just about.

I grab a nondescript bag from his kitchen, and scamper back to the red cabinet.

When I open the drawer, the Cloud glows with an angelic light. Mesmerized, I throw the white wisps into the bag, careful to grab each and every one. There must be hundreds. Enough to last the rest of my short life.

I pull the silk lining until the bare back of the cabinet floor is left. In an act of rancor, I detach Booth's favorite magnet from the fridge and chuck it into the bag. Everyone needs a trophy.

I sneak out the door with a feeling of empowerment. Whoever sees me now, it doesn't matter. Who would care about an eccentric drug dealer? I jump into the street and slip away into a passing crowd.

Someone knocks at the door.

The police, maybe. Finally coming for me.

I adjust my vision to this world. Mika calls my name. Maybe I'm still horizontal, dreaming. The door jiggles, followed by Mika's footsteps.

I can tell by the soft wood creaking that he's in the kitchen. There's a small gasp and I can imagine his face. His nostrils flaring as he encounters the smell of my hovel.

I imagine him making his way through the mess: the sink filled with plastic cups, a dirty blender, plastic measuring cups, empty peanut butter jars. It's been weeks since I've cleaned anything, or had the energy to throw the trash away, so his eyes will scan the kitchen for the worst of the smells Then maybe he will turn to the open fridge, smell the warm pungent invitation of the post-Booth murder cleanout. After visiting Booth's, I threw out my homemade jams, sauces, spoiled deli meat, and pickled vegetables. I chucked the condiments and oils I'd collected and hoarded over the years. In the fridge, I've left only a filter for water, bananas (added protein), and chilled vodka. But I left the pile of bags squished in the bottom two drawers of the fridge after being too tired to take them out, and unhooked the cables. Then he will head over to the sofa, where a bunch of dried throw-up is wrapped in my once-beloved blankets. After a few weeks, it's a smell that can penetrate universes.

If he makes it through all that, will he get to me and my smell? Well—

"Antonia? Wake up." Mika apparently still has some command over my body because I open my eyes and roll over to take him in.

But the sleep is too good. I turn to the cool side of the pillow, letting him come to me.

"My god," he whispers.

I know my face is haggard, but he doesn't have to be a dick about it. He grabs my wrist, taking my pulse. I can hear my own breathing, slow and faint, and wonder how long I've been out. His face fills with concern.

"Wake up."

"Leave me alone."

Mika holds me by the shoulders and cradles me in bed.

I lick my chapped lips as a call for water. I don't know how long we lie like that.

In the morning, I peel myself off his chest and listen to him breathing. He's beautiful like this. Part of me feels we've time-traveled in our sleep, back to a period when waking up to his face was normal. My stomach swells with bloat, a side effect of my terrible diet, but I do not want to move.

I wonder where Hannah thinks he's been. I remember Booth's face, the fear of God that distorted his face when he saw my arms raised holding the rock. I think about how happy I am that I got to do that to him; to show him a fraction of what we felt at Pixel.

"Hey," I say.

He rolls over with those warm hazel eyes. The tip of the duvet obscures his smile. Buried in my skull is the steady hum of guilt, reminding me I'm the one who ruined us, and opened the door to Hannah.

Reckless Antonia, depressed Antonia, the Antonia who called you drunk at 4 am until you picked up, with no concern that you were at your parents' house. I'd hung around bad spaces, an amphibian slipping away from anything good for me. The morning he'd broken it off, I was on a bender. He was already dressed when I got home, morning shift at some local brunch hell spot. We didn't need to say anything. And the months that followed were dark and lonely. Mika set boundaries, moved out, grew up. Eventually, he found Hannah.

And what did I do? Retreated into work. Retreated to a world of misfits. I didn't feel like a freak around people for whom Christmas was any other day on the calendar, who had nothing to do on weekends, who lived for the rush of good food and wine.

I only came back into his life when I knew I could offer him something he wanted: a peace offering named Iris.

The phone rings in the other room and Mika motions for me to hold on.

He slips out of bed, legs heavy, and leaves the spot next to me warm. I think about the last time we were together. He'd just started seeing the girl who would become Hannah, and we were falling apart together, one last time. The sort of decay that lasts days and slips into uneven hours. He'd come back to tell me how their coffee date had gone, and spent his energy on me. I was about to get high, and morality was the furthest thing from my mind. I let him find comfort in me, and cast Hannah in the role of "too good" for him.

When we fucked, my mind went to the buildings in the city. A Mukimono assortment of steel and glass, stripped of its protective skins.

Mika walks back into my room with his shoulders drooped and sits on the edge of the bed.

"I'm feeling better, ready for work," I tell him.

"You can't be serious," he says, finally meeting my gaze.

"What do you mean? I'm good. I slept."

"Babe. You're in no condition. You've lost so much weight. You don't even look like yourself. You're skeletal."

"Wow."

"I just mean—"

"It took me a while to get the hang of this new situation, all this stuff, but I have it under control now. And look, it's peanut butter flavored."

I motion to the old smoothie cups on my bedside table.

"Come on, Boss says time to go. Gimme a ride on that motorcycle of yours."

After some time, Mika mouths the word, *okay*, and helps me dress.

It's a strange dance. Mika cleans me up with a wet towel from the bathroom. He manages to find a clean shirt and some leggings for me to wear. I have to lean on him to put my shoes on, one by one. He's touching me as if I am made of glass, so it takes twice as long to do anything. After I'm fully dressed, he instructs me to drink the rest of his bottled water. It feels good to be told what to do, what to think. If I am no longer a person, maybe I can be a mindless object. I hear the floorboards creak under him as he goes to throw out the trash. The whip of a fresh trash bag startles me awake, and I wonder if I have been asleep all this time.

Once outside, Mika jokes about me falling off, but after a while, a fear descends on his feature, darkening the mood. Instead of the bike, he calls a cab for me. Tells me he will meet me there. Making any sort of muscle movement hurts. I blink twice so he knows I understand.

The taxi cab is unpleasant. A crude fish smell engulfs the car. And the cab driver keeps coughing, releasing spores into the already-decaying car. I left my toothpaste upstairs so I have to swallow back any spit I throw up. The ten-minute ride feels endless. I close my eyes and find a silver lining in my body giving out, in forgetting to fight.

The car whines in front of Iris, where Mika is waiting. I've never seen him look so concerned. It's nice, to have his attention like this. He lifts me out of the cab and lets me lean on him until we go through the staff door.

The crew greets us with silence. The entire staff is surprised to see us together and talks to me like I'm a doll, delicate and hardly able to keep my head up without someone holding me. I couldn't tell if they were more surprised by my physical appearance or by Mika coming in by my side.

The night goes by as it should. In a few hours, I excuse myself to "go for a smoke" and stand in the alleyway, a nibble of cod between my fingers.

Standing very still now. Eyes of a hawk. Cloud's final high is intense, and my inner animal has returned. I creep over to the dumpster and kneel to the ground. Spotted: neighborhood kitty come to dine.

"Psst, psst."

I motion towards the kitty with my fingers, letting it

smell the fish. Then place the fluffy piece directly in front of me.

The kitty is unsure, but this is a good alleyway. It can tell from the dumpster.

Slowly, it leans in, paws first. Pretty quick. But not as quick as my knife.

I'm not a true animal, of course, so I break its neck as soon as it's in my grasp. A cut here and there, and the thing is slowly skinned, much like the deboned fish inside Iris.

Suckle, suckle. The familiar warmth of a fresh kill tastes delectable, pure. Less gummy than the fish, ruddy as a Beijing duck.

I'm picking the meat with the edge of my knife in-between bites when I notice the homeless man eyeing me from his usual spot.

This time, I'm not ashamed. I throw him a bloody grin until he hobbles away.

Thank you for the energy, feral kitty! I slip into my office and jam a couple of ear plugs up my nose, ready to face the evening. Who needs coffee when warm, feline blood is so effective?

The evening is stacked with Friday night reservations, birthdays, and second dates. There's less small talk than usual, and orders are being completed quickly. An occasional "fuck" and burn aid. A ballet of bodies, plates, pots, and simmering delicious things—not to me, but you know.

I'm overseeing the dishes coming out when I feel Lionel's burning gaze from the sink, checking on me, probably at the behest of Mika. I try to ignore this and rush to the serving bar, double checking the last of the plates get properly plated before going out. I mind my station, unaware that the saucepan is burning behind me until Eddie shouts my name.

Without thinking, I grab the wrong end of the pot, and it clunks to the floor.

"Chef!" Again, Eddie.

I take out my nose plugs and am overwhelmed with the grossest stink. How could I forget it. I think of the fresh pig, and look around at the garbage that passes for food around here. It's clear Cloud's sedation has worn off.

"Chef!"

By then, I'm out the door, filled with a purposeful, sudden rage. The world around me spins; changing.

"Don't eat the food! They're poisoning you!" I hear someone scream.

Then I realize the voice belongs to me. I'm standing in the middle of the dining room, a dozen eyes on me, my fever dream, a reality.

I search for an understanding gaze among them, anyone, but the room swirls in shadow and gray. Across the kitchen, Lionel and Mika move in slow motion towards me, aided by a nervous hostess. My eyes bulge, analyzing the horrific embarrassment my new gift has burdened me with. How can they not understand?

Mika's beautiful brown eyes are in my line of sight. And his mouth is moving—though, through my bizarre metamorphosis, I cannot make out his plea.

No one will believe me now. Ah, but did I want this life, anyway? My hiding is getting harder to manage. Short bursts of sanity only keep me in good social standing for so long. Maybe at last, the downhill tumble is accelerating towards the end. Again, the foul odors of the food bubble up to my nose. I make the mistake of glancing at the plates. What miserable nightmares! The walls collapse around me, swaying into the soiled atmosphere of Iris.

And the food—otherworldly, alien, dirty and opaque. Shimmering, always shimmering. Each porcelain plate fills me up with disgust and renders into madness. The bits and globs dance, teasing me with their morbidity.

The room is coming out of shock—overlapping voices of concern, Mika's voice, distorted buzzing, the aroma of the food. Never mind the personal stench of disgrace. I cannot save them.

# A FEAST OF PUTRID DELIGHTS

In the corner of my eye, I see a woman—skinny little thing. Lawyer type, after hours, or perhaps finance. She is trying to ignore the spectacle of the truth. Well, she can try to ignore me standing directly in front of her. I zip to her table and pick up the plate for dramatic effect.

"You have no idea what is in this. They're *killing* you. You understand me?"

The woman lets out a squawk. Her friend across the table pulls her away, like I'm something dangerous. Maybe I am. I throw the plate across the room, or, well, under another table. The break is loud amid the quiet diners.

Mika and Eddie drag me back. Around me, plates of food growl and shimmer mockingly. Vacant stares and shaking heads, patrons pulling out their phones and sending my message to everyone in the world, though their pitiful looks surprise me.

When I come to, I'm in the hospital again. The overhead lights send a jolt of unimaginable pain through my skull. My body is leaden, and there is a weight to my belly. I feel full. I touch the cotton sheets with my brittle fingernails, scraping the cuticles and skin into the fabric.

Machine sounds and phones ring and echo from the hallway. Judging from the strength of the light penetrating the windows, it's the next day.

I'm time-traveling again!

Mika snores next to the window, covered in a lightweight blanket. I roll my neck around to stretch. Then I see it. A thin tube feeding into my body. The pouch droops off the hanger, half empty.

Gray, shimmering contents. Poison.

Agitated, I throw off my covers and grab the line, following the path frantically towards my body. Using my other hand, I cinch the line at one end, trying to prevent any more toxic fluids from entering me. I scratch angrily at the line, which pokes into my stomach. I hiss, and yank at the yellow addendum hugging the feeding tube. I'm just about to get it out when a set of large, hairy hands stops me in my tracks. It's a nurse. I start kicking. Someone grabs my legs. Amir—the look in his eyes pleads for me to stop.

"You're going to make yourself pass out again, Antonia. You're too weak." He stares at me, pleading. Alarmed, I watched the uncinched fluids make their way down the tube. Now it's too late.

Another nurse runs in to help hold me down, followed by a third wielding a syringe. I can only cry, witnessing the gray stuff flow into my body.

"You're killing me. You're killing me."

And the whole room goes black.

The nurse at the checkout counter is a loud middle-aged bitch who I've decided to hate. She eyes me suspiciously with ratty, deep-set eyes. I lean into Mika for support. His shoulder bumps against me as he signs my release forms. He smells like puke.

"Here, open the door," Hannah commands, and Mika follows. I study her neck the whole ride to their apartment. I think about the first time I dreamt of her.

I don't have a good memory of Mika and Hannah's apartment, as I said, so returning feels like deja *blue*. Blue door, there's that. Blue door with the paint peeling near the knob. I'm thinking of the blue door as we're ascending the stairs. I start to think he'll have to carry me. *Goddamn, Antonia. You're so weak*. I think I should just lie here and sleep. What would happen? Who'd come to save me against my will?

When we enter, the floors creak something awful. *Invader*, they seem to say. The house smells like palo santo, chocolate cake, and cedar. Hannah's got them on a new diet. There's green sludge on the counter, moving on its own. I cannot look away. Mika hands me a pair of nose plugs and a glass of water. They've put me in the bedroom, seasonally out of place.

# A FEAST OF PUTRID DELIGHTS

I hear a baby cry near the backrooms.

"Mika." I turn to him, surprised—dazed. "Your baby."

"She was born a few weeks ago."

"Oh!"

"Her name is Claire."

Hannah tenses up.

Hours pass and I haven't moved from the bed. The truth is, I'm afraid to. Creating is bad. The Gift has only gotten me into trouble. There's no perfect meal. I've lost it all, I'm sure of it.

Hannah, effortlessly cool in a band shirt and nylon shorts, pokes into my room with fresh towels. Her short hair bounces with every gesture, heavy rings on both hands that seem to weigh her down to earth, fresh faced with no makeup, but somehow beautiful. Here's an uglier thought: there's a high horse for realizing your own ugliness. I mean *really* seeing, as I can now. As I have been able to since Cloud entered my life.

Hannah gives me a warm smile. I swear she could be an actress. I'd tell her that and mean it, both as a compliment and as a revulsion. She kisses Mika in the hallway when they think I'm not looking.

After an awkward morning, I'm led into the kitchen, which opens into the living space. The apartment is eclectic, lined with book towers and bright acoustic guitars, long framed art resting on the floor, warm light blooming in every corner. There are baby toys scattered everywhere, which make it more endearing. And something else—the smell of milk. The *actual* smell of milk to me. Nothing horrible, or rancid. *Fresh milk.* I stare at Hannah's breasts, suddenly ravenous.

Hannah glides behind the kitchen counter and whirs at a blender. There's something already in there, gray and chunky, with a shimmering film at the top.

"Right, here we are, Toni. I heard you're really into smoothies now."

I manage a smile and Mika clears his throat. The little

bitch knows I detest being called Toni. Suddenly, my face is on the side of some processed goop. I lean in, hiding my disgust, and tell her it looks great. But it's too much for Mika. The two of us here.

He starts, lifting my bag on his shoulder. Hannah glares at him.

"I'm sure she knows where it is, babe." Then turns to me, a grotesque smile again. "First door on the left."

I stay quiet and make my way down the hall. I can almost feel the heat of our tension.

"I thought we were past this—" one of them says. Their voices are so low I can only pick up the vibrations with my feet. Even so, I understand everything.

The room is on the left, as she said, sandwiched between a bathroom and a closet-sized office. I poke my head in and strain my neck to hear.

"Oh yeah, I'm really pleased your unstable ex-girlfriend—who hates my guts—is staying with us, and our *baby*."

Another pause.

"Where is she supposed to go?" he hisses.

"She's an adult. If she doesn't have any friends by now, you have to wonder why."

Then their baby starts crying, and they drop the subject.

In and out of sleep, I hear them bicker.

The medication has made me lethargic. I decide on the second week I'm going to stop taking it.

One evening, when the moon is larval white, the hunger returns. I no longer feel human, but I'm led by a primal sense to their kitchen. Inside the fridge are the usual chef fare—stocks, pastas, sauces, ragu, aged meat. It all smells appalling. Flecks of food from the previous night are speckled all over the counter, mostly messy around the baby's feeding chair.

A predictive hunger swells inside of me.

# A FEAST OF PUTRID DELIGHTS

I couldn't do that.

I open the fridge again and spot the bottles of Hannah's warm milk. Mine, all mine. The liquid is like honey. Sweet and tangy and full of her scents. Better than anything I've ever had, or made for that matter. It's the only thing in this house that's safe enough, pure enough to eat.

After I drink all the bottles, I'm still left unfulfilled. My mind goes back to that perfect pig. I don't have the strength to walk downstairs, to leave the house, to hunt. I need something weaker, something more vulnerable.

Hannah and Mika's white noise contraption hums throughout the flat and I drift aimlessly around the apartment. I follow my nose. Obedient, for once.

A fleshy nameless hunger leads my feet into the room down the hall. What a smell. I can feel the heartbeat, the wonderful purity of that skin, of those organs. Take my hunger, take my tongue, and make me clean again. I kneel in front of the bedroom window, but I know what I must do.

I lean over the cradle, feeling holy and miserable. I twist the newborn flesh and bite down. By the time I hear the screaming, I'm on cloud nine.

# ACKNOWLEDGEMENTS

I could not have done this without the help of the immeasurably talented and wonderful Max Booth, author in their own right and champion of WEIRD. Thanks for believing in me and guiding me through the process. Your dedication to making this a reality fills me with gratitude. And a million hugs to Michael Tichy, author of *The Winnowing Draw*, for your steady friendship and encouragement. Finally and most importantly, I would like to thank my husband, Eldar–sharing this life with you is my greatest gift.

# ACKNOWLEDGMENTS

# ABOUT THE AUTHOR

Valentina Rojas is a writer whose work delves into the forsaken and the unknown. Her recent work can be found in *Ghoulish Tales, Coffin Bell Journal*, and *Mouthfeel Fiction*. A graduate of the University of St Andrews with a degree in International Relations, she's been seeking redemption ever since. When not crafting her web of horror, Valentina can be found working in games or haunting the Rockies with her partner and their three dogs; Zelda, Olivia Souffle, and Toast. This is her first novella.

## Connect with Us: